# THE BURNTWOOD
MEN

# THE BURNTWOOD MEN

ROBERT MCCAIG

CUTTING EDGE

ISBN-13: 978-1-952138-49-2

Published by
Cutting Edge Books
PO Box 8212
Calabasas, CA 91372
www.cuttingedgebooks.com

# 1

---

THE CHUNKING of the *Mountain Queen's* sternwheel walked rhythmically across the water. Her whistle mourned, the sound striking back from the high cutbanks across the Missouri. Tam Barrie walked along the levee as the *Queen's* blunt prow bent toward the bank. He could hear the jangle of her bells as, with her paddlewheel turning dead slow, she followed her bow wave almost into the bank. At the last moment her reversed wheel flung up a flurry of white water. The *Mountain Queen* was safe in Fort Benton, at the end of her long journey from St. Louis.

Tam Barrie stood among the crates and casks, the bales and hogsheads piled in gross confusion on the Fort Benton levee. He watched as a hundred eager hands reached for the boat's mooring lines. As the deck hands ran the stage-plank out, he moved forward. If Dove Demarest and Cleland Strike are on her, he thought, no use in waiting. I might as well let Strike know a representative of the bank is on the job, even if it does rouse that devil's temper of his. And I'll see Dove, maybe have at least a word with her.

Passengers began to stream down the stageplank in a flurry of handkerchief waving, of cries of greeting, of sobs and embraces and confusion. Tam moved close to the water's edge, where he could scan the face of each passenger. The main press reached the levee; the crowd on deck thinned. Then Cleland Strike came striding down the ramp.

Tam's heart leaped. There was an elemental brutality in Strike that had always made the short hairs bristle on the nape of

Tam's neck. He felt—well, that the man was never quite a gentle-man. There was too much violence in him. He came down the stageplank now with his air of arrogance unabated. Tam moved forward around a mountain of crates.

Strike saw him. He took the last step to the levee, frowning a little.

"What on earth—you here, Barrie?" he asked.

Tam nodded. "On business for Seaboard & Continental. I want to meet with you, Strike, at the very first opportunity."

Strike stared at him. "All right, all right, tomorrow, then. At my place. Though I don't know why—never mind. Run along now, Barrie. I have business afoot. Don't get in my way." There was the finest edge of threat in the words. Cleland Strike swung around, his broad back toward Tam, the corded muscles strain-ing the fine broadcloth.

Tam, irritated, stepped back. He turned to see Dove Demarest coming down the stageplank.

She's as lovely as ever, he thought, watching this distant cousin of his as she came down the ramp with her lilting walk. Imperious, headstrong, wild as a prairie hawk, she had never seemed in fear of man or devil. A good trait, Tam thought, if she's thrown in her lot with Cleland Strike. They'd damned well better be married, he thought grimly, or I'll ...

He was close enough to catch the words of Strike that answered that question, at least.

"Good morning, Mrs. Strike," Cleland said.

"Good morning, Mr. Strike." She tucked her hand under his arm, laughing up at him. He patted her hand, and said some-thing in a low voice that made her laugh anew. Though she did not look in Tam's direction, he suddenly felt the urge to get away, finding the thought of facing her unbearable. He stepped back, almost bumping into a group of bystanders.

"Land sakes," a gaunt frontier woman said, touching the fresh cheek of a young woman passenger, "Nellie, I jest cain't believe it's you. So growed up and all, and married to sech a handsome husband. I'll bet this place don't look like shucks to you, Nellie. Well, it's mighty rough, and life in Montanny Territory ain't never easy. But you'll find it a good life, child, you wait and see. Purty soon you won't want to trade Benton fer a whole passel of Keokuks."

"I hope you're right, Aunt Bessie," the girl said. "But this country's so *big...*"

Tam moved away, knowing how she felt, meeting the raw force of this wide and ugly land. There was a struggle awaiting the girl, and anyone else who tries to tame even a small corner of it. So different from the settled graciousness of the land he had come from.

Tam took a turn up the levee, swinging back to where he could see Dove and Cleland talking to the captain and the mud clerk at the foot of the stageplank. Pity he couldn't have his conference with Strike immediately, though he knew there'd be no chance of his taking the *Mountain Queen* downstream tomorrow. She was making a fast turnaround to avoid being caught by lowering water, with July well along. Tam had been told there would be other boats later, but after this spring rise had ebbed, none of more than threefoot draft. No matter—even a keelboat would do if it would take him out of this God-forsaken country the moment he had completed his business with Strike.

Most of the passengers had gone from the levee. Tam threaded his way among crates of machinery toward the foot of the stageplank, hoping for a way to watch Dove without being observed, for he still wasn't ready to talk to her. But he didn't approach within hearing distance of the group, for a gentleman didn't eavesdrop. He saw them look toward the head of the ramp.

A man came unhurriedly along the deck. He paused at the top of the stageplank, with a flair for drama. Tam watched him, finding him an interesting figure. His skin was a dull bronze, his hair black, and he wore plain dark clothing, except for a bright

3

Assomption sash twisted around his middle. As the man came down the ramp, Tam saw that he had an ascetic face, the cheekbones high, the lips thin and mobile. Here, Tam thought, is a man who has subjugated the flesh to his own discipline. Not large in stature, but with a power in him, some inner light of dedication or fanaticism, whatever the name men call it. Here is a man who will sway the emotions of other men.

"LaCroix!" Strike called. The man paused, then came on down the stageplank. Strike asked him something, and LaCroix shook his head. He pointed toward the street, and the two men hurrying toward the boat. Tam saw that they were dark of skin, with an Indian cast to their features. Their jackets were fringed buckskin. They wore dark trousers and a kind of legging made of heavy wool decorated with designs in colored beads. Like LaCroix, they wore the gay Assomption sash. They greeted him with deference.

Strike turned toward them, laughing, and said something to LaCroix. The man drew himself up haughtily. He turned away. Flanked by his two men, he strode up the levee to River Street. Strike stood staring after him. Even at this distance, Tam could sense the pure malevolence in Strike's manner. He was so intent that Dove plucked twice at his sleeve before his tense pose relaxed and he turned back to her.

He offered his arm. Without hurry, they strolled up the levee to the street. A carriage drew up and stopped, the driver saluting Strike with a gesture of his whipstock. Effortlessly, Strike lifted Dove up into the carriage, and sprang in after her. The driver cracked his whip, and the equipage rolled away in a cloud of dust.

Tam reached down and picked up a scrap of pine wood. With his jackknife he whittled long shavings from it, venting his impatience. He should have insisted that Strike talk to him immediately. But, damn it, you can't make a man settle down to business at the end of a long river journey. Tomorrow Strike would have his feet on the ground. And he had better have some answers, Tam thought grimly. He slashed the stick in two and tossed the pieces into the turgid water. Closing the knife, he started toward River Street and the town beyond.

He had to talk to Strike. He had learned little in Fort Benton, partly because of the cautious nature of his preliminary inquiries. Besides, while the language purported to be English, it was filled with prairie argot with meanings lost on his unaccustomed ear. And these people were close-mouthed with strangers. He hadn't even established to his own satisfaction that Strike had a ranch set up to receive his cattle drives. He shook his head, knowing that questioning on that point would arouse the man's explosive temper.

I've been sent here, Tam thought dourly, to lock stable doors: my reward for being the only one in Seaboard & Continental to oppose the loan to Strike. No matter that it was partly because I don't like the man, I did oppose it. So I'm the one sent across the prairies to the edge of nowhere to safeguard the loan. One hundred and fifty thousand dollars, on the flimsiest of security, mainly the word of Cleland Strike. Clee Strike can talk, no doubt about that. Talk? Why, he had those golden herds of cattle thundering right through the board room. The directors could fairly smell the dust of the driver as he spoke. And being related to the insurance Strikes hadn't hurt his cause. The directors had patted him on the back and handed him the money and off he had gone to the West, Dove Demarest with him.

Tam's fingers went to his cheek, feeling the scarce-healed scar Cleland Strike had put there. Suppose the directors had known he hated Clee Strike's guts—would they have sent him West? It didn't matter now. When the belated reports had begun to come in about Strike's shady enterprises and odd entanglements, the directors had given Tam his instructions: See that Strike launches a successful cattle operation, or bring back the money, intact.

Even at the time he had thought it a large order. But he had jumped at the chance for several reasons: It was an opportunity to take a step forward in his work, and such a break did not come often to a junior clerk. It was a chance to vindicate his judgment concerning Strike. But primarily (and the admission was with some self-contempt) he was concerned for Dove Demarest. He had loved her once. He must still love her, to have traipsed clear across the country after her, and she loving another man. Still, he couldn't forget.

He turned down Front Street, the soft dust puffing up around his boots. Dove could always wrap me around her finger, he thought, from the time I was a studious and proper small boy. She walked over me, and laughed, and I came back for more. She used me that night, asking me to escort her, knowing it would make Strike wild with jealousy. Not that I didn't know it too, and ran the risk. But she made not the slightest move to intervene when his superior power and weight made my lessons in the manly art of self-defense a joke. She made more over Strike's black eye than over my broken head and sprained shoulder. But still I worry about Dove. She is like a drug in my blood.

He kicked a rock in the road, taking pleasure in the way the shock of it tingled up his leg. He walked north, toward the sign of the Centennial Hotel.

Cleland Strike, at the bottom of the stageplank, said with some impatience: "Ah, LaCroix, here you are at last. My carriage is coming. I've got a cabin back of my house where you can stay."

LaCroix shook his head. He said, in his deep, resonant voice: "My thanks. But my people await me at their camp beyond the town. Here are two of them to take me there."

Two men in Métis costume came hurrying down the levee. Strike stared at them, not offering a greeting. He said to LaCroix: "Better change your mind. I'd feel honored to have as a guest the John Brown of the half-breeds."

LaCroix drew himself up as if he had been slapped. "M'sieu Strike, my people are not curs or mongrels. We are men—we are the Bois Brûlés—the Métis."

"Don't get owly, LaCroix," Strike said, an edge of warning in his voice. "Our interests are tied together too closely for anything like that. I was trying to pay a compliment. Make our meeting tomorrow, then. Two o'clock at my house."

"I may be there. If things go well—if I am ready for talk." LaCroix said shortly. "I shall send a messenger. Au'voir, m'sieu', madame." He touched his hat and walked away, his two men flanking him.

Strike stared after him, his face dark with anger. He said: "That half-breed son of a bitch better not get uppity with me. I'll have his black hide before …"

Dove plucked at his sleeve. He saw her patent disapproval.

"I beg your pardon, my dear," he said, patting her gloved hand. "I was carried away—forgive me. Ah, there's our carriage. Come, I'll give you your first glimpse of the Strike mansion."

He offered his arm, smiling again. Going up the bank, Dove had to take two steps to his one. The driver of the carriage saluted sketchily with his whipstock, grinning down at them. Strike put his hands around Dove's slim waist and effortlessly swept her up into the carriage. Laughing, he sprang after her. The driver popped his lash. The team lunged; the carriage rolled away in a rattle of loose spokes and a creak of unoiled leather.

Away from the riverfront, they turned left at Arnoux Street. Strike's arm was around her, pulling her close to him. He stopped her breath with a long, hard kiss. She was gasping when she pulled away. She put up her hands to straighten her flowered hat.

"Clee! What will your townspeople think of such indecorous conduct?"

"They'll be jealous, no doubt," he said. He tried to pull her close again.

"Clee, stop! You'll wrinkle the only decent gown I have. That is, since we went off without my trunk."

"I'll have Lisbon Frank pick it up at the boat," he promised. "Dove, stop worrying. You always look like a picture from *Godey's Ladies' Book*."

"But will your friends think so if I'm all mussed up?"

"I have few friends in this benighted wilderness. All of them will think you're a damned pretty minx, and they'll spend two-thirds of their waking moments trying to figure a way to get you into their beds."

"Clee! The things you say! The driver—"

"—had damned well better see nothing and say nothing. And he knows it," Strike said with a certain coldness. "My dear, don't begrudge my friends their dreams. That's all they'll have. I guarantee to monopolize your attention, awake or asleep."

"My, how we brag," she said archly. "But, Clee, I do love you. You took me by storm, and I haven't recovered."

"That should teach those Philadelphia dudes to treat women like women, and not marble statues on a pedestal. Like that moonstruck cousin of yours, Tam Barrie. By the way, he's here."

"In Fort Benton?" she asked in surprise. "Tam here? What does he want? Clee, promise to treat him kindly."

"Of course—unless he crosses me. Which he could, seeing he claims to be here on bank business. He'd better not forget that lesson I gave him last winter."

"No, Clee! You were brutal that night. Tammie is a dear boy, and I—I more or less led him on."

"You think I didn't know? Barrie is a grown man, Dove. I took the only way to teach him that when Cleland Strike puts his brand on something, other men keep their hands off. Barrie is not the first to learn that, nor will he be the last."

Respect, almost fear, was in Dove's glance. "I had no intention of criticizing my husband," she said.

"Good. So if Barrie wants to keep a whole skin, tell him to stay away." He tightened his arm, almost crushing her ribs. "Here we are—the family estate."

The residences along the street had been for the most part one-story cabins, the yards narrow behind whitewashed picket fences. Strike's home was of two stories, painted white, with green shutters. It had a faintly Colonial air under the gingerbread and scrollwork of its ornamentation. There were trees and shrubbery in the yard. The carriage stopped in the gravel driveway.

"Where are all the family retainers?" Dove asked, laughing.

Strike reached up his arms and swung her to the ground.

"Call 'em that if you want," he said as they went up the steps. "Lisbon Frank, here, driver and handyman; Kilgore, the broken-down old hostler; a couple of boozefighters Con Aleff and Dirty Nose Smith, who help out occasionally; Bryce Flinn, out at the ranch; and the 'breed housekeeper, Sophie Valier. She's no jewel, but help is hard to muster out here. A word of warning, Dove. Don't cross Sophie. She's independent as a hog on ice."

He lifted Dove and carried her across the doorstep. Laughing, they went into the parlor. Dove saw that the house was poorly kept, a film of dust on the heavy furniture, lint and fuzz under the chairs. She felt a small shiver of disgust, but said nothing. Clee Strike, she had learned, disliked criticism of anything that was his. It aroused his smoldering temper, and Dove had found it expedient not to waken that temper if it could be helped. The sudden flaring of it frightened her.

"The house is—is cool and pleasant," she equivocated, working the fingers of her gloves free.

"It's dirty as a pigpen," Strike said, scowling. "Sophie! You lazy Métisse slut! Come in here."

A solidly built, handsome woman with jet hair and coppery skin appeared at the door of the parlor, soundless on moccasined feet. "W'at you want, Strike?" she asked sullenly.

"A little respect, and this place clean," he said. "Sophie, this is my new wife, Dove. You do what she tells you. I want this place mucked out, y'hear? You got my note. Is the big bedroom ready?"

"Bedroom all ready, bed clean," Sophie Valier said, her eyes as black and expressionless as polished coal. Soundlessly as she had come, she faded into the hall toward the rear of the house.

"That insolent baggage," Strike said. He ran his fingers over the top of the rosewood piano, scowling at the marks in the dust. He rubbed his fingers with his handkerchief. "It's your chore to train that woman, Dove."

"Though I'm neither cook nor housekeeper, I'll do my best, Clee," she said. "Will you take my bag upstairs?"

"In a minute. Glad to be here, Dove?"

"A little frightened," the girl confessed. "I'm so ignorant about so many things. Clee, I don't even know how you make your living, though I know it's in some kind of finance."

He laughed. "Finance it is. If you're worried, my dear, I assure you that we are not on the verge of starvation."

"Of course not," she said with dignity. "But I wondered—Clee, why is this man LaCroix so important? You talked to him all the way from that landing where he came aboard—Carroll, was it?—to Fort Benton, and you have more meetings to come."

He took her slender wrist between thumb and forefinger. He bore down with his amazing strength. Tears sprang into her eyes.

"Listen, darling—this is a business matter. A very secret and touchy one, as you might gather. What you don't know won't hurt you. Moreover, remember this from now on—the business of Cleland Strike is his business, and his only. It is not to be told in Gath, or published in the streets of Ascalon. That lovely rosebud mouth of yours is to be kept closed, you hear? At all times, no matter what the compulsion."

Her own temper flared. "I'm your wife, Cleland Strike. From the moment we were wed, your business became my business.

So I want to know what is so secret about the cattle business, the money for which was a loan from my father's bank."

He shook his head. Reaching out, he pulled her hard against his chest.

"That cattle story served to pump $150,000 out of Seaboard & Continental," he said. "But, Dove, my dear, that story was for public consumption. The whole truth would frighten you to death. Just believe this, Dove: stick with me, ask no questions, keep your mouth shut, and you'll wear diamonds." He gave a short bark of a laugh. "Perhaps even a crown of them. Who knows?"

"What if Tam Barrie finds out …" she began.

"Tam Barrie is greener than grass, and a nincompoop besides," he said, releasing her. "He'd better go back. The Whoop-Up country will eat him alive."

She picked up her gloves, moving irresolutely toward the door. She started to speak, but Strike was lost, staring out of the window. Disturbed by his strange manner, she went slowly up the stair, to find the privacy of her bedroom.

# 2

MOVED BY some inexplicable whim, Tam Barrie had made concessions to the customs of the frontier. He had discarded the stiff bowler battered by the long journey across country. He had purchased a new Buckeye Stetson. He had trimmed down his bushy mustache to a narrow line. Looking in the mirror, he was quite pleased by his rakish appearance. Picture of a Fort Benton dude, circa 1880, he thought. He grinned at his reflection, slanted the Stetson a shade more toward the right side, and went out of the hotel.

On Front Street, outside the Centennial, Tam hesitated. His course should be to brace Cleland Strike at the first possible moment. But, he thought with a sudden pang of jealousy, Strike might not be up yet—nor Dove. He must choose his moment, for his inquiries around town had indicated that Strike was not a man to be handled with impunity. Tam had found dislike for the man, and veiled criticism, but even among his critics there had been grudging respect. Unless he were in the right mood, Strike would enjoy annoying or evading Tam. And certain questions must be answered, if it took Tam all summer.

Irresolute, Tam stood watching the crowds. In spite of his lack of rapport with the raw crudity of this land and the people who lived in it, Tam was stirred by the swing and the sweep and the hurry of it. Here was lusty life, primitive but exciting.

He saw muleskinners and teamsters, tomorrow outbound on the Whoop-Up Trail, who would turn northwest to Fort Macleod or east to Fort Walsh. Here were hide hunters and wolfers, the stink of them so rank that men walked wide of them on the street. Yet they themselves seemed inordinately proud of their stench and their lice. Here were full-blood Indians, preferring white men's garbage to the scrawny beef of the reservation, now that the wild cattle, the buffalo, no longer blackened the plain from the Larb Hills to the Big Hole.

Now two men of the Métis passed Tam, in their colorful costumes, trim with a French flair, even to the fringed sash around their waists. Strong, straight men, who smiled with a flash of white teeth, their manner alert and confident. Their name for themselves, Tam thought, fitted them well, for their skins were a glowing dark bronze: the Bois Brûlés, the burntwood people.

Tam moved on down the street. In the noise and the color of Fort Benton, he drew a contrast with Butte City, two hundred miles to the south. That town was wild enough, and raw enough, but it lacked the special flavor of Fort Benton. He had spent some time in the smoky little mining city, on his way here. Not of his own wish.

Racing west by train and stage from Philadelphia, Tam was trying to arrive in Benton ahead of Strike, who had embarked, Tam had learned, on a river steamer at St. Louis. Somewhere between Corinne, Utah, and Butte City, Tam had picked up a fever. Perhaps in one of the verminous stage stops, perhaps from some fellow passenger. By the time he reached Butte he was racked by chills, and shaken by a cough that tore at his insides. Pure luck dropped him into the hands of a rawboned jade who ran a boardinghouse. Annie Callaghan had a whisky breath and a heart of gold. And she wasn't going to have a dom' Protestant dyin' in her house. Consequently with goosegrease, hot rum, and profanity she had nursed and cajoled Tam back to a semblance of health. He had been some time convalescing, so long that he had arrived in Benton just three days before the *Mountain Queen* docked.

Thinking of Annie Callaghan, thinking of others he had met in this hodgepodge of races and peoples, Tam admitted a reluctant fascination. The moment his mission for the bank was completed, either in success or failure, he would depart for the East by the first means of transport that came to hand. But he felt the pull of this town, the odd power it had to move him with excitement. It was so new and strange to him, so different from what he had known, it frightened him a little.

He walked down to the levee, watched as the *Mountain Queen* finished loading her bales of hides and stinking stacks of robes, and saw her pull away into midstream, to disappear around the long bend to the north. He walked back to Front Street. With a sudden decision, he turned west on Arnoux. Strike's temper, he thought, will not improve with age. He did more or less agree to meet with me today. Might as well get it over with.

He looked at the two-story house with interest as he approached. He had been told that it was built by Grandison Strike, Cleland's father. The elder Strike was buried in an unmarked grave somewhere along the Teton, having earned his untimely demise by insisting to a drunken Black-foot brave that one beaver plew was good for just one drink of watered-down trade whisky and no more. Grandison Strike had been one of the last of the free traders, those ephemeral links between the mountain men and the great trading firms of this day. The new traders were businessmen who liked to be called "the merchant princes of the prairies."

Tam went up the steps, and knocked. After a moment, a 'breed woman opened the door a crack and peered out at him.

"W'at you want?" she asked.

"Tell Mr. Strike that Tam Barrie is here to see him."

"Mr. Strike not home. Mrs. Strike, she here."

Tam's heart jumped. "Ask her if she'll see me," he said.

"You wait," the woman said. "I find out." With a soft pad of moccasins she was gone, leaving the door ajar.

When heels clicked on the stair, Tam deliberately turned away, pretending interest in the buildings of Benton, and the sweep of the river beyond. The steps came closer, the door creaked slightly. Tam turned.

"Why, Cousin Tam!" Dove cried. Her arms went around his neck. Her lips were soft and warm on his. For a moment the soft firm curves of her fine body pressed against him Then laughing, she thrust him away. "Tam, let me look at you. Clee said you were here, but I can't believe it. Come in the house. Clee is out, but he should return soon. We'll have a chance for a good talk."

He followed her into the parlor. "My best wishes on your marriage, Dove," he said.

"And how relieved you sound that I *am* married," she said, "and not living a life of sin. Yes, Tam, Cleland and I were married in Chicago on our way west. And—he's wonderful, Tam."

"Glad to hear it," Tam said brusquely. "You weren't very considerate of us at home, Dove. But then, you were always a law unto yourself even as a child. I suppose you lead Strike around by the nose, just as you did me in the old days."

There was an impish gleam in her eyes. "No, Tam. Not Cleland Strike. If you don't know by now that no one leads him, you'll learn, and it will be a hard lesson. But I did lead you, didn't I? We had fun in those days, sweet coz. Remember that rainy day in the loft of Grandpa's barn when you tried to fondle me, and I hit you on the head with a pitchfork handle?"

Tam's face reddened. Unconsciously his hand went to the back of his head. "And well I deserved it," he said, "though you had teased me like a wanton until I … But that's an old, lost time, Dove. What of the present? Are you happy?"

He sensed a shadow of hesitation. Then she said: "Of course, Tam. Supremely happy. Everything is new and exciting, and Clee adores me. No regrets, Tam."

"Good," he said, meaning it. "I'll probably see you often in the next few months."

She arched her eyebrows in surprise. "Is that discreet, Tam?"

"On business, I mean," he said. "I'm out west in the interest of Seaboard & Continental."

"Papa's bank? Concerning the money they loaned Clee?"

"You know, then. They want to know if the range cattle business is a likely field for further investment. They intend to study your husband's operations in some detail."

"Your old money matters are not my province, Tam. But here comes Clee now. I hear him riding up."

She touched him lightly on the cheek. He flushed a little, hearing the tinkle of her knowing laugh. He turned toward the door.

Strike came into the parlor, beating the clinging dust from his hat against his knee. His eyes narrowed as he saw Tam.

"What are you doing here, Barrie?" he asked, his glance flicking sideward to Dove.

"We had a business appointment, remember?" Tam's voice was businesslike; he tried to ignore the anger that welled in him from the very nearness of the man.

"I conduct my business affairs at the store of Strike and Company," Strike said curtly. "Now get out."

Frowning, Dove moved to her husband's side. "Clee, don't be unreasonable. Tam represents the bank. Give him a few minutes."

Strike scowled. "I know, the bank is worrying about their $150,000. Not badly worried, though, or they'd have sent someone more important than this office boy."

Tam held his temper. "That's how office boys get to be vice presidents, Strike. They want me to investigate this range cattle business of yours. Some of the directors are beginning to question your figures. My job is to see if you are as good at cattle raising as you sound. I'll admit you did a good job of convincing them there was money to be made, perhaps too good a job, for they sent me out here to verify your claims."

"What do you know about the range cattle industry?"

"Nothing. Our western correspondents agree, however, that with the buffalo vanishing, there will be grass for immense herds of cattle. You borrowed the money to bring in those cattle."

"And I will. But I arrived just yesterday. Do you and the bank expect me to conjure great herds out of thin air?"

Tam shook his head. "Of course not, Strike. But the season is well along. The bank expects me to follow your progress, to see that you use their loan wisely. There have been rumors—"

"What kind of rumors?" Strike growled.

"The bank has its confidential sources in Washington and in Ottawa," Tam said. "We even have access to the confidential reports of the Royal Northwest Mounted Police. And the police don't like Strike and Company. According to their files, you were active for years running whisky across the border. They say you smuggled furs and robes. They have a report that last year three wagonloads of guns and ammunition filtered across the border, to end up at Sitting Bull's camp in the Cypress Hills."

"What is that rumor to me?" Strike asked.

"Just that it was Strike and Company that supplied the arms, and Strike and Company that ran them north. Further, Strike, there is another rumor, a vague one, hinting at something deeper."

Strike took out his cigar case. He selected a perfecto with elaborate care. He clipped the end, and lighted the cigar with a lucifer. He got it drawing exactly to his liking. Though a drift of blue smoke, he gave Tam a cold and speculative look.

"Isn't the range cattle business deep enough? Isn't it precarious enough a gamble to occupy a man?" he demanded.

"The bank thinks so," Tam said. "But there was the persistent whisper that out here on the far prairies some dangerous and treasonable game was afoot. And there's nothing more cowardly than big money, Strike. So they sent me out here."

Strike gave that harsh bark of a laugh. "So they thought I'd be fool enough to jeopardize my future, use their $150,000 to gamble? Well, suppose that rumor were true, Barrie. What would you do about it?"

"Our bank has power in high places, Strike," Tam said slowly. "Power in Washington, where our government at the moment is very sensitive about Canada, with Sitting Bull crouched just across the border. And we have power in Ottawa, where Sir John Macdonald is not unaware of the need for funds for Dominion development, especially for his dreamed-of transcontinental railway. The reach of Ottawa and Washington is a long one. This frontier is not without law."

"You'll find it mighty damn' seldom," Strike said.

"There are troops at Fort Shaw, Fort Ellis, Fort Assiniboine, even a small detachment right here," Tam said. "And the U.S. Marshal, Mr. Biedler, could receive orders for an investigation. Very heavy pressure might be placed on the two banks in Fort Benton, even though you are a heavy stockholder in one of them. So you see, Strike, if the cattle business develops as you promised the directors of Seaboard & Continental, they'll support you to the utmost. But if you are engaged in some deep and perilous game, I'll have to unleash the not inconsiderable resources of the bank to safeguard our loan."

Strike rubbed his chin, staring hard at Tam. "Big words, Barrie. Petty personal revenge is on your mind. I suppose you've already run tattling to Biedler."

"Of course not," Tam said. "I'm not going to turn any hounds loose until the scent is stronger. I don't claim there is anything to these rumors, Strike."

"Of course there isn't," Strike said curtly. "I'm an honest cattle drover, a trader, a beef raiser. My father and I may have stepped out of line a time or two in the old days, but damn it, a man had to. It was root, hog, or die, back then along the Whoop-Up, in the time of the whisky traders and the Spitzee cavalry. But I can see fortunes to be made legitimately out of this cattle business. You can watch me day and night, Barrie, if it gives you pleasure, and you won't catch me out. I can't say I care for your cold nose sniffing into my affairs, but since you are on the side of money, I suppose you can call the tune."

Tam felt a surge of triumph. He hadn't supposed it would be so easy. "You don't like me, Strike. I know that," he said. "I like you no better. But this is business—you keep to your contract, and I'll not interfere. And that's a bargain. One other thing— your wife, Dove, is my cousin. See that you treat her kindly."

Strike threw back his head, laughing. "Why, good for you, rabbit," he said. "Dove, you run to Tam when you have a tale of woe. He'll horsewhip me on the front steps, no doubt." His tone changed. "All right, Barrie. You've had your say. Now get out!"

Tam was far from satisfied, but he realized that further talk was useless right now. He felt that he had prodded Strike into action, action that had been strangely lacking, as far as his inquiries could develop. He bowed to Dove, wondering about the look of concern on her lovely face. Taking his hat, he walked out of the house.

# 3

WHEN TAM was gone, Dove said, "He's a dear lad."

"He's a fool," Strike said. "But he's in a position to be damned troublesome." He began pacing the parlor like a big cat.

"Clee, there isn't any truth in what he hinted?"

"Why, my dear, not a grain, a dram, even a breath. But it annoys me to have idiots interfering with my careful plans."

"I could stop him in a minute," she said archly.

"With a touch, a kiss, some half-promises of delights that might be his? Wouldn't it be fun, playing that game, my dear? With me here to hide behind if you took one step too far, and the rabbit got ideas?" He reached for her, pulled her hard against his hard chest. "Leave it, Dove. I'm enough man to absorb all your coquetry and your less ladylike moments. I'll handle Barrie."

"Clee, you wouldn't hurt him?"

Strike shook his head. "I wouldn't lay a hand on him. But I'll fix his wagon, for all of that. He needs a lesson."

Later, Strike went out the back door and down the path to the log bunkhouse edged against the hill. Three men were playing cards at a deal table. They didn't bother to finish the hand.

"I'm surprised that you had the guts to come back here, Smith," Strike said coldly.

The big man, shaggy as an unkempt bear, seemed ready to cry. "I didn't go to do it, Mr. Strike," he whined. "But that dam' Injun kid needed killin'. At that, I jest had my knife out, ticklin' him a little, when he moved sudden …"

"Small loss, but it makes talk in the town," Strike said. "But I'll give you a chance to make it good. There's an Easterner in Benton, name of Tam Barrie..." He gave terse, clear orders. "...and don't fail me, Dirty Nose. Make it tomorrow at sundown. You botch this, and I'll have your gizzard, raw."

"I won't miss, Boss," Dirty Nose Smith said.

The dark man, Lisbon Frank, spoke then. "This pilgrim carry a six-shooter, Mr. Strike?"

"No. But we can remedy that." Strike took a little pistol, almost a toy, from his pocket. "Frank, you take this. After Dirty Nose has downed Barrie, you be the first to reach the body. Slip this into the dirt alongside him. Con, you cover it from the sight of the crowd. Then Dirty Nose can say Barrie drew on him."

Con Aleff nodded. "Is the little peashooter loaded?"

"Call it a peashooter if you like," Strike said. He pointed it at the dirt floor in the corner of the cabin and pulled one trigger. The noise crashed in the small room. He handed the pistol to Lisbon Frank. "Makes quite a hole at close range. It's a forty-one caliber double derringer. Frank, always watch the little points. Now one barrel had been fired. You can patch up a story from there."

Tam ate a late breakfast. Afterward, he walked through the musty lobby of the Centennial, past the desiccated rubber tree. On the porch he stood picking his teeth with a quill pick, looking down the street. The July heat was oppressive, but it did not slow the teeming traffic of Front Street. Tam tossed the toothpick away and went down the steps. He shouldered his way through the press until he reached the Benton National.

The banking room was empty and quiet, in contrast to the hurly-burly of the street. Beyond the wooden railing that divided the room, Aran Hausbird, the cashier, worked at a desk. He dropped his work and came forward as Tam reached the railing.

"Mr. Barrie, I'm happy to see you," he said. He glanced nervously around. "Give me your letter of credit," he said in a low tone.

Tam looked at him, puzzled. Since he had presented his letter of credit his first day in Benton, he had gotten to know Hausbird. They had enjoyed their shop talk, comparing the free and easy ways of frontier banking with the operations of a great firm like Seaboard & Continental. He had learned to respect the man.

He did not hesitate. He handed the cashier the letter of credit. Hausbird disappeared into the strong room. He returned with a sheaf of greenbacks and a sack of coin. He dumped gold pieces from the sack, counted them with swift expertness, and dropped them back into it. He flicked through the bills, penned notations on the letter of credit. He knotted the string around the neck of the bag and handed it to Tam, with the letter.

"Put this inside your coat, and hide it," the cashier said. Relief was visible on his face.

"There's trouble in the air?" Tam asked, putting it out of sight.

"I can smell it," Hausbird said. "Caldwell, our bank president, asked about your letter of credit, first thing this morning. I told him you'd drawn on it. He scowled at the ceiling, hemming and harrumphing like the old walrus he is. Then he hurried out. I can read the man like a book. When he gets back, he'll have orders not to honor your letter of credit any further."

"And whose will be the orders?" Tam asked.

"A certain powerful merchant. The grapevine has it that you have offended Cleland Strike. Strike just happens to be one of the biggest stockholders of the Benton National." He flicked a thumb toward the bulge of the moneybag under Tam's coat. "But ahead of those orders, you have enough cash to keep you from being broke or stranded. For a while, anyhow, unless you let some disciple of Jesse James relieve you of it."

"I'll take care of it," Tam said. "My thanks, Aran. You're a real friend. Hope it doesn't get you in trouble. I could have presented the letter at the Miners' and Drovers', down the street."

"You'll find Strike calling the tune there, too," Hausbird said. "No, cash is safest, Mr. Barrie. Just so the rough element doesn't learn of it."

"I won't tell them," Tam said, smiling. "Because I would be easy meat—I can handle a rifle a little, or a fowling piece, but I'm scared to death of these short guns, In this land of experts, I'm better off unarmed, I figure."

"Perhaps you're right," Hausbird said. "But be careful." He reached across the railing to shake Tam's hand. "Good luck, Mr. Barrie. You'll need it—Strike is a powerful enemy."

"He's not a new enemy, Aran," Tam said. "And I *am* afraid of him. Still, I'd give a deal to know just what he's up to—I have a hunch it isn't cattle ranching, as he claims."

"There are rumors, but they are vague and formless. If I get any definite word, I'll try to let you know, Mr. Barrie."

"Do that, Aran. I'm a stranger in a strange land."

Hausbird gave him a knowing smile. "You're not a babe in the woods, Mr. Barrie."

Leaving the bank, Tam wished he could agree with the young cashier. But Hausbird's words gave him a warm glow, for he seemed to be the only person in Montana Territory so far who thought Tam Barrie had sense enough to come in out of the rain.

He cut through the alley and up the back stairs of the hotel. In his room he took enough cash from the sack for his personal needs, and buried the sack under dirty clothes at the bottom of his small trunk. He had been told that in this land of violence, burglary and theft were relatively rare, perhaps because such strong measures were taken against them. Tam hoped so. He did not trust the strongbox of the hotel, and besides, Clee Strike might own part of the Centennial also. Best keep the money close.

Now, since Strike, in spite of his implied truce yesterday, had made an overt move against Tam Barrie, Tam felt no qualms about coming out in the open to check Strike. The business card of Seaboard & Continental opened to him the counting rooms of the leading Fort Benton merchants, but these men were guarded in their answers to questions he tried to keep discreet. All of them agreed that Strike had made much talk of driving cattle from Oregon; that he had set up some buildings on land he owned in the shadow of the Highwoods, a quarter-section of patented land with good water; that Strike had registered a brand, *Rafter S*, with the local Association. Two of the merchants considered Strike's plan a wise one, predicting that several similar operations might start soon, possibly with their hands in the financing.

Concerning Strike personally, Tam could get little satisfaction. These men, he felt, did not consider the trading methods of Strike & Company either admirable or ethical. But they would only hint that Strike was an exploiter, an opportunist. As for Strike's claim that he was hiring cowboys, they said quite a few men had been coming into Benton, inquiring for Strike, and shortly thereafter moving on. A grizzled trader said: "Cowboys— maybe. But they sure as hell didn't look like no cowpokes to me!"

When Tam ended his quest and turned toward the hotel, Front Street was much quieter, the long shadows of evening slanting across river and road. Things don't fit well, Tam thought, as he went down the street. Strike should have his herds well on the way to Montana by this time, but he seems curiously inactive. Tomorrow, he decided, I'll find a guide and ride to this so-called rancho of Strike's. I'll look it over for myself.

Ahead, from a saloon door, a man came lurching, the batwing doors flapping indecisively behind him. The man fetched up against a porch post and leaned against it, cursing. He was big, surly, ragged, dirty. He pulled a pistol from a worn holster and dangled it from a big hand. He did not look back toward the doors.

Because he had no real reason to retrace his way, Tam walked on toward the man. The man brushed futilely at the dirt on his dirty shirt, and spat, and looked up slyly at Tam. His eyes were empty, not even surprise in them. His lips curled back from broken, yellowed teeth. The hand with the pistol raised.

The pistol came to waist level. The muzzle pointed at Tam's belly. The corded thumb drew the hammer back. Shocked realization came to Tam. He read the hot eagerness that now filled the man's empty eyes, and he knew, with stark horror, knowledge that was past belief—*in the next few seconds this stranger was going to kill him where he stood!*

No use to run. He saw the pistol center, the man's hand shaking a little. Tam came up on the balls of his feet, his one desperate chance, he thought, to rush the man.

Down the sidewalk someone yelled: "Dirty Nose! Here I am, damn you! Turn around and take it!"

The big man lurched, and wheeled away from Tam. In an eyewink the street exploded in a yammer of gunfire.

A bullet ripped a long gouge in the plank at Tam's feet. Behind him, the window disintegrated in a jangle of broken glass. The door slammed shut. Tam jumped out into the street, a spout of dust geysering from the roadway behind him.

At the street edge stood a watering trough, its planks green with ooze. Tam flung himself behind it, unmindful of the mud and slime. A bullet chunked into the wood, and Tam clawed himself flatter against the ground, feeling the rasp of dirt harsh against his skin. His heart was thudding with excitement. Keep your head down, he warned himself. This little war shouldn't last long, and this is as safe a place as any.

Above him, running feet pounded on the walk. A shot crashed, another. Men yelled. Then something heavy and lately alive pitched across Tam. Tam tried to slide from under, but could not without getting from behind the barrier. He twisted his head to look.

The big man who had held the pistol leered at him. He was grotesquely dead, half his face shot away. Good enough, Tam thought. But the warm wetness that was seeping out of the man, ruining Tam's clothing, brought sudden revulsion. Tam retched into the dirt of the street. He twisted around, reaching, trying to lay hands on the pistol the man must have dropped.

Again feet on the sidewalk above him, running, stopping. A laugh like the bark of a dog, no amusement in it.

"Here's Dirty Nose. The son of a bitch is dead."

"Good enough. Who's the fool layin' under him?"

"Looks like the pilgrim that's been hangin' out at the Centennial."

"Good God! Hope he didn't stop any lead."

Tam felt the sodden weight of the corpse hauled off him. Rough hands jerked him to his feet. He stood up, his legs trembling.

"Is the war over?" he asked, trying to grin.

Five men, as tough as the one who lay dead. They stank of sweat and tobacco. They stood there, grinning back at him.

"What's the matter, sonny, wet yer pants?" a bearded man asked.

Feeling moisture, Tam brushed his hand against his trousers, wondering for a moment if he had. His hand came away wet with bright crimson, new blood, not his own. He felt the nausea rise in him again, and turned quickly to the watering trough. As best he could, he scrubbed hands and face in the scummy water, and with his handkerchief he mopped the stains from his clothing. He balled up the handkerchief and threw it away. He faced the men.

"Hain't ye never seen a deader before, pilgrim?" the bearded man asked with a note of sympathy in his voice. "This ain't likely to be your last one, if ye stay in Montana Territory."

"Then I hope they're not all as messy as that one," Tam said. "Who killed him?"

"Why, I did," the bearded man said in some surprise. "Me, Colly Devoe. And not one dam' minute too soon, say I. What was Dirty Nose throwin' down on ye for?"

Tam shook his head. "I never saw the man before in my life."

"Ye hain't? He was within an ace of puttin' a slug through ye. Well, I had enough reasons for killin' the coyote. Who might ye be, son?"

"Tam Barrie. Late of Philadelphia, U.S.A."

Devoe reached out a hand like a gnarled root. "Howdy, Tam Barrie. Are ye in funds? Then mebbe we could honor your narrow escape by havin' something' to cut the dust outen our throats. At your expense?"

"You saved my life. Will all of you join me in a drink?"

"Why, here's a sport. But not in this hog troft. The Buckhorn's jest down the street."

"But what about—that?" Tam jerked a thumb toward the crumpled heap of rags that had lately been a man called Dirty Nose.

"Say, that's right. Brock, run over to the sheriff's office and tell Johnny Healey we left him a corpus to plant. If'n he tells you to go to hell, jest let Dirty Nose lay and jine us at the Buckhorn. Dirty Nose won't git no riper'n what he was when he was alive, and that's a gut. Come on, sport."

A solid small man extricated himself from the group and trotted away. The others started up the street toward the Buckhorn, the word "The pilgrim's buying!" running ahead of them. So Tam and Colly Devoe entered the saloon at the head of quite a motley crew of drifters. They lined up at the long bar.

"Whisky," Tam told the bartender, tossing a double eagle onto the bar.

# 4

TAM GULPED his drink. Harsh as it was, it eased the spasms of his stomach. He refilled his glass, enjoying the adulation of these rough men, though he knew it meant nothing beyond a device to keep the whisky flowing. But it pleased him to hear a man say, "Doggone, the pilgrim's all right!"

The man Brock elbowed his way up to the bar. "Healey's away," he reported. He grabbed a bottle and spilled whisky into a glass.

"Off chasin' hoss thieves somewheres, I guess," Devoe said. He picked up bottle and glass and turned away from the bar, motioning the other two to follow. At a table at the far side of the room he sat down, motioning Tam to a barrel chair beside him. He splashed liquor into Tam's glass.

"Have another, Barrie," he said. "You'll find death parches a man's gullet, if you had a hand in it or no."

"I hate to think of that—that corpse lying in the street," Tam said.

"I tole Sappington, the depitty," Brock said, taking a chair on the far side of Tam. "He said he'd git a team and wagon and haul Dirty Nose away. Another pauper fer Chouteau County, he says."

"He'd better be on the county," Devoe said. "Johnny Healey ner Jedge Tattan neither better look fer me to pay the shot for the buryin' of Dirty Nose Smith. Killin' him came under the headin' of public benefaction. Damned if I'll pay fer the privilege."

Tam was appalled. He had never met callousness and ferocity of this kind. Mayhem and murder and sudden death did not seem to touch these men. Yet he was finding in himself an odd envy. An educated, mannered man like himself should feel only disgust at these unwashed, whisky-swilling frontiersmen. Instead, he felt himself the outsider, and envied them.

"Why were you looking for this man Dirty Nose?" he asked Devoe.

"You glad I found him? Well, I'd had enough of him. While back, he done me dirt in a hoss trade. Then he stole a jim-dandy blacksnake of mine out of a wagon, and sold it. Now, them ain't killable misdemeanors, so I let 'em go. But yestiddy this Injun kid, cousin to Shadbolt's wife, was foolin' around in the alley back of Strike's store. Dirty Nose worked there sometimes. They was some kind of a ruckus, Dirty Nose claimin' he caught the Injun kid stealin'. So he slipped eight inches of Bowie between the kid's ribs. Shadbolt's wife, she's out by my place at the Métis camp, jest a-cryin' and a-carryin' on something awful about this dead boy. I come to town, and Brock met me and tells me Dirty Nose had called me a son of a bitch. That done it. I hunted the skunk out and killed him."

"Killed a man, just for a bad name?" Tam asked, unbelieving.

"Why, sure. I ain't claimin', mind you, that Maw and Paw ever had preacher's words said over 'em. Ner that Maw was always as choosy as she mought have been. But that don't give Dirty Nose no right to say such here on Front Street. On top of that—the Injun kid, he was a thief and a liar, and lousy besides, but he was better'n Dirty Nose, by a damn' sight. So Dirty Nose, he didn't have no call to gut the kid."

Tam shook his head. "It beats me. For a hard name, a man dead."

The bearded man shrugged. "Barrie, here in the Whoop-Up country a man ain't got much *but* his name, whether she's real or jest one he made up. Or one he borried from his betters." He filled Tam's glass. "Drink up, Tam. That gang of reperbates is looking' over here, hopin' you'll treat ag'in. Let 'em look. If you buy more, they'll think you're a plain dam' fool, even while they drink your whisky. O' course, me'n' Brock here, that's different. We'd like to sit and drink your liquor all night, given the chanst. Eh, Brock?"

A good chance to end it, Tam thought. I don't intend to get these men drunk or to get drunk with them. He stood up.

Instantly, Devoe was standing at one side, Brock at the other. With gentle insistence they shoved him back into his chair.

"Now, there's no hurry, son," Devoe said. "This soldier here"—he held up the bottle—"is only two-thirds dead. And you still ain't told us what you're doin' out here in the Whoop-Up, that somebody wants to kill ye fer."

Tam stared at the man. Was he already drunk, that he was talking nonsense? Finding a motive in the senseless brutality of an insane man. Why, he had to get away from these violent men …

Devoe put a hand on Tam's shoulder. "Now, hold on, young Barrie. I apologize. I didn't have no call to ask ye that question, nor do ye need to answer. Wa'n't no proper way fer me to do. But it's like this—me'n' Brock are lookin' fer work. We had hoped to ketch on with the big Diamond R train that left yestiddy fer Fort Ellis. But we didn't make it. So it jest come to me—here's a pilgrim all by his lonesome with some renegade gunnin' fer him. He might be pleased to hire a pair of good lads to ride shotgun, as it were."

"Guard my person, you mean?" Tam asked. He saw the big man nod. Tam sipped his whisky. It might be an idea he thought. God knows I could use some kind of help. If could trust them …

"What can you do?" he asked.

Colly Devoe looked at Brock. The little man chuckled. The big man leaned back and laughed, a stupendous, gut-shaking laugh, the more remarkable because it was almost silent.

"Why, Tam Barrie," Devoe said, leaning forward, his forearms on the table, "I wouldn't be jokin' if I said we kin do dam' near anything. Betwixt the two of us, we got a tol'able knowledge of this country. We come to Pembina in the fifties, and we been movin' west ever since. Benton was jest a pup when we come here in '68. We've sashayed all over the Injun country, and that was in the time before the smallpox trimmed 'em down. We crossed Piegan country and Gros Ventre; we've traded with Blood and Crow and Sioux and Northern Cheyenne, and by God, we still got our hair! We been trappers an' wolfers. We skun mules and whacked bulls and broke hosses. Jest one thing I ain't done, ner Brock neither. We never shot buffler from a stand."

He looked at Brock. The little man nodded solemnly.

"I married a Métisse," Devoe went on. "She's dead now, God rest her soul, but our daughter is Métisse too. Mebbe that's why I hate the hide hunters, the way they've killed off the Injuns' cattle, the Métis' walking grub supply. But outside of that, me'n' Brock have been to hell and back. We've rode from Cheyenne to the Cypress Hills, and from Coeur d'Alene to Milestown. I've seen whisky ladled outen a barrel, through a slot in the stockade of a wood fort, until a whole tribe, brave, squaw, and papoose, was stretched out like dead outside the walls. We was with Johnny Healey when he made the Spitzee cavalry turn tail. Tam, you name it, and from Fort Macleod to the Hole-in-the-Wall, there's dam' few places where we ain't heard the jackass bray. Nor have we took backtalk from any man, red nor white."

Tam nodded owlishly. The saloon seemed oppressively hot and smoky. He stood up, swaying a little. "I'll think it over," he said, finding his tongue clumsy. "Think I know the hand back of this. If it hap-happens again ..."

"If it happens ag'in, you may be dead," Colly Devoe said. He drained his glass. "Mebbe, if we was workin' fer you, we could persuade this gentleman he ought to mind his manners."

"I have my doubts," Tam said. "From the way people act in Fort Benton, he's one big important man, is Mr. Cleland Strike."

Brock's chair rasped back. "You heard him, Colly," the solid man said, wiping his sleeve across his lips.

Devoe nodded and stood up, his face serious. "We been braggin', son. We'll take it kindly if you fergit we had this little talk. Thanks fer the whisky."

Tam said with contempt, "You scare easy, for such big talkers."

Devoe nodded. He looked around the crowded room. He said "I tell you, son, the *Margaret Hilda* casts off at dawn. If you're smart, you'll be aboard her. Because the Whoop-Up ain't no place fer a man who cocks a snook at Clee Strike. Nor is me'n' Brock anxious to be seen in the company of sech, because we might end up the same as him—and that's with our Goddam' heads blowed off."

Brock snapped his fingers. He said: "That's it, Colly. You mind that Dirty Nose Smith was Strike's man, most times?"

"An' I killed him," Devoe said slowly. "When he was on orders to salivate Barrie. Son, you ain't got no time to wait fer no *Margaret Hilda*. You should be gone on the high lope right now, and the two of us with you."

"They wouldn't tackle us right here on the streets of Fort Benton," Tam demurred, feeling cold beads of sweat spring out on his face.

"You think they'd give a damn?" Colly asked. He turned to look toward the door. His face hardened. "They ain't even bidin' their time. See the two that jest come in, them standin' at the end of the bar? Lisbon Frank and Con Aleff. Strike's men, both of 'em. And they're packin' iron."

Tam looked down the bar. The two men looked ugly, mean, and dangerous. A feather of panic touched Tam's spine. He looked squarely at Colly Devoe. "You're up the creek, just as I am, Devoe," he said. "So how about you and Brock taking that job you asked for? Right now."

Surprisingly, Colly Devoe chuckled. "Good fer you, Tam. Well, we're right ram spang in the middle of her. Might as well git paid fer it, eh, Brock?"

The solid man licked dry lips. But he nodded assent.

"All right, Tam Barrie. You do like I say. An' don't make no mistakes. In a minute or two, Brock and me will stagger out the front door. You give us three minutes. Then you head fer the back door, like you was lookin' fer the privy. We'll meet you out in the alley."

"But ..." Tam began.

"No 'buts,' " Colly Devoe said sharply. "It'll take them two, five, ten minutes to fire up their Dutch courage. They ain't in no hurry. You act half full of booze, and they'll take their time. Look sharp now, Tam. Here we go."

Tam watched the two lurch across the room, arm in arm. His heart was thudding, but nobody paid any attention to Devoe and Brock. Even the two men at the end of the bar gave them little more than a glance. Tam watched them stagger through the batwings, out into the summer night.

He held his place, though the impulse to run was strong. He gulped his whisky, shoved the empty glass aside, and rested his head in his hands, his elbows propped on the table. From the corner of his eye he saw the two men turn to look at him. Just then a newcomer entered the saloon, a burly man, muleskinner by the look of him. He threw an arm about the shoulders of Aleff and the Portuguese with the friendly clumsiness of a big bear.

Tam slid away from the table, cat fast and cat sly. He was at the back of the room and into a dim corridor, running along it in dim lamplight. He found the back door. His heart leaped in panic when it wouldn't open. He jerked harder, and it gave. He slid through, and shut it softly behind him.

The night was ebony. Blind, Tam stumbled down a plank walk. Gradually his eyes adjusted to form and meaning. The low cube of an outhouse, a fence beyond it—once whitewashed, enough left to give it luminosity in the star-shine. He opened the gate, cursing the creak of it. He listened, poised for flight, hardly breathing, feeling his ears twitch with the very intensity of their straining. There was only the night clamor of the town, an indistinguishable hum of sound.

Neither sight nor sound of Devoe and Brock. Never should have depended on them, Tam thought. Here he was in the dark, the stinking dark—the night air of Fort Benton a miasma of smells, a veritable explosion of odors. The flat smell of warm dust, the sour reek of stale beer, the sick-sweet stink of sewage thrown openly into street and alley, other odors even worse, all compounded into one mephitic assault on nostrils and throat.

A voice said from the dark, "Don't dawdle, Tam," so close that Tam jumped. Devoe's voice, so it must be Devoe's vise of a hand that grasped Tam's arm. Just then the rear door of the saloon was flung open. Tam felt the hand tighten. Men burst from the oblong of yellow light in the bulk of the building.

"Hurry, Tam," Devoe said, turning him.

Tam tried to run. Instead he blundered into a pile of tin cans. He went sprawling amid a hellish clatter and clangor. He tried to scramble to his feet, fell again. He heard Devoe curse. From the saloon yard gunfire flamed, lead snapped overhead. As Devoe dragged Tam to his feet, a lighter gun from the alley answered the shots from the yard. A man yelped.

"Brock's holding 'em," Devoe panted. They pounded down the alley. "Tam, you take out fer the hotel. Throw enough gear together fer a week or two. Meet us in the alley back of the Centennial in five minutes." He gave Tam a shove. "Move, lad, the whole town'll be out here in a couple of shakes!"

Tam went away from him. He dived into a cross street. Two blocks over, he turned behind the buildings. His thoughtful landlord had left a lighted lantern hanging at the back entrance of the Centennial. Tam pounded up the outside stairway. He burst into the dim hallway, lighted by a single bracket lamp. Fumbling for his key, he got his room open. He relocked the door from the inside and with shaking hands lighted the lamp.

He ripped off his filthy clothes and donned clean ones. Shoving extra trousers, shirts, underwear, and essentials into a big carpetbag, he thrust the money in on top of them. He grabbed a storm coat, tossed his spare gear into the trunk, and slammed the lid. Then he blew out the lamp, and left, not bothering to lock the door behind him. The hall was still empty; so was the outside stair. On the bottom step he paused, listening. From the darkness came the twitter of a night bird.

"Colly? Brock?" Tam called softly.

"Git to hell out of that light and over here, you idjut!" Colly Devoe growled.

Disgusted at his own stupidity, Tam scuttled across the alley to where Devoe stood, a dim shape at the edge of the lantern glow.

"Run, Tam," Colly said. Tam sprinted down the alley, Devoe keeping just behind him, seemingly with little effort. Their footsteps were soundless in the powdery dust. They came to the end of the alley and turned north. The moon broke through the thin overcast. House and store, tree and shrub sprang into weird, unreal shapes. Tam had no idea where he was.

Colly slowed down. "Nobody behind us," he said. "Soon as we git to the livery barn, we'll pick up hosses and hightail it out of town. Those tough hoodle-ems won't give up easy."

Through weedy byways they came to a high rail fence.

"That you, Colly?" Brock called out.

"Yeah. You got the hosses?"

The solid man materialized out of the night, leading three horses. He thrust reins into Tam's hand. "You ride, kid?" he asked. "Cain't guarantee how gentle this critter is—or ongentle."

"I've done some," Tam said. He reached for the stirrup. The horse shied, and Tam heard the snap of teeth just beyond his shoulder. He swung up into the rocking chair of a stock saddle, odd-feeling and heavy after the English pads he was used to, as a gentleman rider of fair ability.

"Didn't git you, eh?" Brock chuckled. "Watch him, Barrie. No hoss likes to be woken up in the middle of the night."

"Can't say I blame him," Tam said. "Let's go."

As they moved out, he heard Brock tell Devoe: "I writ a note fer Perky sayin' we borried this sorrel, will pay up later. Else the dam' fool would be runnin' to Johnny Healey sayin' the hoss was stole."

"You did? Perky can't read," Devoe said.

"Dam' if that ain't so," Brock said. "Well, let Perky go to Healey then. A man ain't got no more gumption than to stay ignerant, he's a dam' fool anyhow." He dropped back, and they turned into the lane, riding Indian file, Tam in the middle.

Tam followed Colly Devoe, the man big against the feeble stars. The moon kept sliding in and out of the ragged overcast. The weird soft lights was more deceptive than darkness. Tam gave up trying to find landmarks, and was content to follow Devoe without argument. They left the buildings, and skirted the end of a hill. The trail wound through brush. To his right Tam saw the glisten of stars reflected in the black of the river.

The trail broadened. Colly stopped long enough for Tam to catch up to him.

"My shebang is about seven mile north of the town," he said. "You'll have to stay a while, for in my 'umble opinion, in Fort Benton your hide ain't worth a plugged nickel."

"The natives proved hostile," Tam said.

"Dam' if they didn't," Devoe chuckled. "We'll have Brock keep an eye on the town. Mebbeso things will cool off."

They topped a small knoll. Off to the right the red glow of campfires reflected from canvas and tanned hide. Devoe stopped, looking toward them. Tam and Brock ranged up beside him.

"The Métis camp is stirrin' like a kicked ant hill," Colly said.

"Had another big council, most like," Brock said. "I hope none of 'em git so het up their trigger fingers itch."

"You scairt of 'em?" Devoe snapped.

"Colly, don't be so tetchy," Brock said angrily. "I know they're your adopted people. I like 'em my own self. But you got to admit they're owly as all hell these days. Some young fire-eater could git spooked and empty a Winchester at the sound of us."

"Well, ride soft, then," Colly Devoe said. "We turn off here, anyhow."

They rode around the shoulder of a great hill, the faint silver sheet of the Missouri behind them. In a pocket among the trees stood a cabin, yellow lamplight outlining a window. Beside Tam sounded the liquid notes of a hoot owl's cry, so lifelike that Tam jumped.

THE CABIN door opened and light stretched out across the worn grass. The door remained empty.

"Is that you, Papa?" came a girl's cautious voice.

The owlhoot sounded again. The girl hurried from the doorway, a rifle held ready against her slim body. She ran towards the riders. Colly Devoe swung down from his horse. He caught her up in a great bear hug, rifle and all. Then, with his arm around her, he started for the cabin. Over his shoulder he said: "Brock, take care of the hosses, will you? Tam, grab your possibles and come along."

Dismounting, Tam untied carpetbag and coat, and gave the reins of his horse to Brock. The solid man rode off, trailing the two horses, whistling a nameless tune softly to himself. Tam walked into the cabin, blinking in the lamplight.

The size of it surprised him. This was a room of hand-hewn beams, at the far end a great stone fireplace, and around the room low benches and chairs grouped at random. Hooked rugs of bright colors decorated a floor of rammed earth as smooth and clean as terrazo. At the end opposite the fireplace, another door appeared to lead to other rooms. At one side a vertical ladder led to an attic opening.

There was pride in Colly Devoe's voice as he said, "Tam Barrie, this is my daugher Stephanie."

Tam blinked. The girl was a lovely thing, her dark eyes startled and shy. There was a hint of copper in the gold of her skin; her hair was the blue-black of a crow's wing feathers. She stood poised lightly, as if to take flight at the first hint of danger. Color suffused her cheeks under Tam's frank stare. She dropped him a quaint small curtsy.

"How do you do, Mr. Barrie," she said. "Papa says you will be staying with us for a few days. You are welcome; our home is yours."

Before Tam could answer, her father said: "Ain't she a jim-dandy, Tam? Brung up in the mission, this girl. And then she went two years to the Sisters in St. Looie. She kin read anything, an' cipher. She kin cure the sick, an' a dozen other things. But she wasn't too proud to come back to keep house fer an old reperbate like me."

"I'm Métisse, Papa," the girl said, with a touch of pride. "Walls of stone and brick are not for me. Nor the crowding of hundreds of strangers. That's as much the reason I came back to the prairies as the fact that you can't get along without me."

"What did I tell ye, Tam? Stevie, I'm glad you keep that rifle handy. This young feller got hisself in a mort of trouble in Benton—no fault of his. Some tough lads are on his trail. They might come here."

"They had better not," she said. "Papa, tell the truth, now. You were in a fight, weren't you?"

He nodded, his face serious. "A bad one. I kilt a man, Stevie. Dirty Nose Smith, the one that let daylight into Shadbolt's wife's cousin yesterday. He was about to shoot Tam, cold blood."

Tam looked at the girl, waiting for the horror of what her father had done to touch her. But she shook her head sadly, her face grave, not seeming shocked at all.

"You won't be in trouble over it, Papa? Good. I'm sorry it had to be your hand that killed that Smith beast, but someone would have had to do it sooner or later. What he did to that Indian boy was cruel, pointless murder."

"Nobody much will miss Dirty Nose," Devoe said.

"Maybe Cleland Strike," Tam said.

The girl gave him a quick glance. "That's right. I think Smith was one of Clee Strike's men. Is there a pattern in this?"

The inflection of her voice as she said Strike's name puzzled Tam. There seemed to be an undercurrent of hatred in it.

"Afraid there is," Colly admitted. "Tam got hisself on Clee's blacklist. And since I stepped in, there's likely a bullet or two with my name carved on 'em. Oh, well, I been shot at before."

Stephanie smiled. "And been missed, mostly," she said. "But be careful, Papa. Strike's men are dangerous. Now, I know that whenever you've been courting trouble, it makes you hungry. I'll fix some food for you and Mr. Barrie." With quick graceful steps she went through the door at the far end of the room.

"Cain't figger it," Devoe said, watching her. "How an ugly old coot like me could sire a girl like Stephanie."

"She *is* beautiful," Tam said. "I would think she'd be married."

"She's had beaus by the dozens. But she don't encourage 'em. Says I'm her favorite. Y'see, her ma—God rest her—died when Stevie was jest a little tyke. So fer twenty year, barrin' the time she was away at school, I've raised her. Pretty much boy-fashion, I'm afeered. She kin ride an' shoot and trap; she kin cook too, by damn. I'll tell you, Tam, Stevie kin take care of herself in any company."

"You must have been a very young man when your wife died," Tam said. "But you never married again."

Devoe grinned. He shook his head. "Leastwise not with bell, book, and candle, as the feller says. It's like this, Tam—once ye been married to a Métisse, any other woman looks mighty paltry to ye!"

Dove Demarest Strike smoothed a lace shrug around her shoulders and looked at herself approvingly in the cheval glass. She swung her body, watching her reflection, loving the knowledge of her own beauty. It pleased her for its own sake, over and above its efficacy in charming her husband. She arched her back, admiring the thrust of her fine bosom. She adjusted the throat line of her dress to show even deeper the enticing cleavage she had so carefully managed. Smoothing the sleek silk down over the curve of her hips, she took a final glance at her reflection, smiling at herself over her bare shoulder before she left the room.

In the parlor, she settled herself against the horsehair of the sofa in a conscious effect. Picking up a magazine, two months old, she leafed through it. The styles, she thought, are changing. The lines more simple, the ruffles and furbelows fewer. But they are going stark mad about the bustle; it is becoming so enormous it will be unmanageable. Still, the styles will do well by me. How lucky, to have a real woman's figure, not needing hip pads or bust pads! I'm a conceited wench, she thought, smiling at herself. But a girl can be smug about natural gifts that other women envy.

There was a knock at the front door, but Dove did not rise. The 'breed woman padded past the parlor door to answer, as Dove had shown her. Dove tossed her magazine aside, leaning forward to hear the low-voiced colloquy at the door. She could not make it out. When the door closed and footsteps came down the hall, she took the magazine again, looking up from it to the two men who stood with some uncertainty in the doorway of the parlor.

"Why it's Mr. LaCroix!" Dove cried. She came gracefully to her feet. "Sophie, for heaven's sake bring them in. Then make a pitcher of cold lemonade and bring it here."

The woman stared at her, spat out a short guttural that might have been assent, and left. Dove thought she saw a faint smile on the ascetic face of Pierre LaCroix. It irritated her.

But she did not show it as she indicated chairs. This man held some key place in the plans of her husband. It would be well to butter him up, though he was a half-blood.

"So nice to see you again, Mr. LaCroix," she said. "But I do not know your friend."

"An associate, Gabriel Valier," LaCroix said, inclining his head toward the powerfully built, grizzled man with him. Valier gave her a courtly bow, but his eyes were unreadable.

"Mr. Valier," Dove murmured. "You wished to see my husband, Mr. LaCroix?"

"Rather, he wishes to see us," LaCroix said stiffly.

"He did not mention an appointment to me," she said. "But then, I find business so puzzling, Cleland tells me little of his affairs."

"Good," Valier said, a gleam of malice in his clear gray eyes.

Dove bridled. "Why, Mr. Valier, shame on you! I think women keep secrets as well as men."

"Women have no secrets," Valier said. "Even among the Métisse—"

The entrance of Sophie interrupted him. She carried a tray with a pitcher and three glasses. She looked helplessly for a place to put it down.

"Over here," Dove said sharply.

The woman lowered the tray to a table beside Dove. The heavy pitcher slid sideways. Sophie made a wild grab for it. It overturned, dumping a flood of sticky liquid into Dove's lap.

Dove sprang up, holding the soaked fabric away from her. Her lovely dress, the first time she had worn it! For Clee. Sophie, concern on her dark face, tried to dab at the stains with a cloth.

Dove slashed the back of her hand hard across the woman's cheek. "Get away from me, you—you ignorant animal!" she cried. And on the instant she realized what she had done. But it was too late to mend.

The woman flung the damp cloth on the table and stalked from the room. Dove, still holding the wet dress away from her body, looked at the two men. Her heart sank. There was disdain and anger on the narrow face of LaCroix. Valier was looking away, his iron face set and harsh. Both men were standing.

"—I'm sorry," Dove said uncertainly.

LaCroix said stiffly: "Your husband can come to our camp, if he wishes to talk to us. We do not come through doors where our people are not welcome."

Dove hurried after them to the front door. She made a final plea. "But, gentlemen, I didn't mean…"

Valier turned with a sardonic smile, white teeth gleaming in his bearded face. "Madame Strike, you do not even bother to learn the name of this woman you slap and call 'animal.' But she is Sophie Valier, sister to me, Gabriel Valier." He turned his back squarely on her and strode across the yard to where LaCroix waited in a buckboard.

Dove changed her ruined dress. She was sitting in the parlor when her husband came in. "Sorry I was delayed," he said. He looked around in surprise. "Where are they?"

"LaCroix and Valier? Gone home, I suppose," Dove said.

"Dove, you little fool, did you do something to them? Those men are damned important to me. Come, let's have it."

She told him, dabbing at her reddened eyes with a scrap of lacy handkerchief. At the end of her story, she moved closer to him, looking up, expecting his forgiveness.

His stormy face frightened her. It was more than unforgiving. It was almost cruel. He pulled her against him with a grip on her upper arm so strong that she cried out.

"Dove, I warned you. I won't warn you again. You act the fool like this and you can ruin everything I have at stake. From now on, stay clear of my affairs. All of them. Keep your mouth shut, you understand? shut, about anything you see or hear or even speculate. Your sole duty is to warm my bed. You have no part in my business affairs."

"I was only trying…" she wailed.

"I know, I know. And I suppose I can patch it up with those stiff-necked fools, since they need me as badly as I need them. But Dove for the love of God, use some discretion. And first of all, go and apologize to Sophie Valier."

"Me, apologize to that half-breed slut?" she cried.

The flat of his hand cracked across her cheek like a gunshot. Dove staggered. Strike grabbed her by the shoulders, pulling her against him.

"Dove, I won't be crossed!" he said through clenched teeth. "That woman is the key to Valier, and Valier is second only to LaCroix among the Bois Brûlés. Get out in that kitchen now. And do the thing right!" He gave her a shove away from him so that she staggered.

"Clee, you don't love me!" she sobbed. "If you ..."

"Git!" he said harshly.

The highbred daughter of the Philadelphia Demarests was not used to eating crow. The humiliation of it almost choked her. But in the end she established an uneasy truce with Sophie Valier, and the woman agreed to stay. In her own bedroom afterward, Dove wept softly in the bitterness of her shame. And a faint touch of fear, for this woman was not one to have for an enemy.

She heard her husband's heavy tread on the porch. Going to the window, she saw him walking toward the bunkhouse. As she let the curtain fall back, she felt a sudden accession of terror. What manner of man was this she had married?

# 6

T AM BARRIE and Colly Devoe had been hunting deer. Or, more accurately, Colly had been hunting, for Tam was unarmed. On the height of land that turned the Teton north to join the Marias a few short yards from its junction with the Missouri, Devoe had downed a spike buck and a barren doe. Now the men were heading back, the deer gutted and lashed to the pack horses.

"You ever try venison liver, Tam?" Devoe asked. "It eats good. But it don't keep, so we'll light down and make our nooning on it."

They halted in a grove of great cottonwoods beside the river. Tam gathered dry sticks for the fire while Devoe prepared the meal. When the fire was blazing well, Devoe threw a handful of green leaves on it.

"That might keep down the dang mosquiters, maybe," he said. "I'll call you in a bit, Tam, when the meat's ready."

Tam, sweating in the windless heat, cast a longing glance at the green waters of the river. He started shucking his shirt. "That water looks good, Colly," he said, stepping out of his trousers. "I'm for a swim."

"Why, say, I begun to notice my March bath is wearin' off," Colly said, slipping his galluses from his shoulders. "A man does git a mite gamy this hot weather, I'll jine ye."

Tam liked swimming. It was his prime athletic accomplishment. He swam with a long overhand stroke, outdistancing Devoe, who used a powerful, surging breast stroke, looking like a sportive walrus. Tam was still idling in the water when Devoe tired and swam to the bank. Knee-deep in the water, the older man scrubbed down his torso and legs with sand.

Tam watched, floating on his back in the cool water. He shuddered at this Spartan substitute for soap. The man's tough, he thought. And thewed like an old grizzly. Funny how white his body is when face and arms are so dark-tanned. Those scars that crisscross the great muscles of thigh and back—I wonder where he got those? And that pink dimple on his shoulder is a bullet wound if I ever saw one.

The older man rinsed himself off and clambered up the bank to get into his clothes. Tam lazed in the water a while longer, until the delectable odor of cooking meat drifted to his nostrils. He came out and raced up the bank, hurrying into his clothes without even drying his body, for the dry air blotted up moisture in minutes. He grabbed pan and fork and found a seat where the smudge had driven the mosquitoes away.

Afterward, when they had packed the gear and ridden south, Tam said, "Best meal I ever ate." And meant it.

"Told you that'd eat good," Colly said. "Besides, Tam, hunger makes a right good sauce. Back there in Philadelphi-a you'd turn up your nose at sech provender."

Remembering the way he had wolfed the fried liver and afterward wiped his greasy fingers on his trouser leg, Tam grinned. "There was a day," he said. "But now I don't know if I would."

As they rode on south, the afternoon heat was as heavy as a blanket. Colly talked little, and, deep in his own thoughts, Tam was as silent. He fell back into speculation and worry about his assignment for the bank, and how badly he had botched it. But the bank couldn't have guessed that its agent would be turned into a hunted man, running for his very life. Nor at the moment did Tam see any way to move against Cleland Strike. The man was too powerful. He came back to the same conclusion—best to lay low a while longer, among these good friends he had found.

Thanks to Aran Hausbird, Tam had the cash to pay for sanctuary. If he could get the Devoes to take anything, which he doubted.

He was reminded of a question that had been nagging at him. He spurred his horse alongside Devoe.

"Colly, a lot of people seem to hate and fear Clee Strike. But your daughter appears to have a deep and enduring loathing of the man. Why?"

The plainsman gave him an odd look. He hesitated, then said: "You'll find out sometime. Two years ago, when she come back from school, my girl was jest half an hour from marryin' Clee Strike."

"The hell she was!" Tam jerked out.

"Gospel truth. It was a bad thing, because the kid was in love with him. But she found out he was married already. Stevie took it mighty hard."

"Married already? Does his wife still live?"

"Fur as I know. Little Cree gal. She had a child by him. Her old man put a rifle to Strike's gizzard and marched him to St. Peter's Mission. Lives up by Batoche now, they say."

"Then Dove…" Tam began. Then, with all the sincerity of a man who was seldom profane, he cursed Strike, his ways and his works and his antecedents, going back now and then to cover a point he had missed. When he had finished, a curious emptiness in him, Colly Devoe looked at him admiringly.

"Tam, I don't believe I ever heard the subject covered better or more thorough," he said. "I'm sorry, too, fer the leetle gal that thinks she's married to him. Didn't know she was a relative of yours."

"A cousin of sorts," Tam said. Here was a deeper quandary. The truth would crush Dove. He knew that she must not learn it from him, or she would, with woman's logic, never forgive him. Nor would she, right now, even believe it. Another of those things awaiting solution, charged against Strike's account. "Someday there'll be an accounting between me and Cleland Strike," he told Devoe. "We seem fated to come to violence."

"I'm with ye, Tam," Colly Devoe said. "This thing of Stevie has gnawed at me ever since it happened. But she made me promise to let sleepin' dogs lie, though it was against my instincts. He hurt her cruel, Tam, and I hate his guts."

"She's a proud woman," Tam said, thinking too of Dove.

"Stevie is that. She is Métisse. Some folks call the Métis half-breeds, but that ain't so. Lots of 'em don't have more'n a drop of Injun blood, but they're proud of it. Like Stevie's ma—she was half French, a quarter Scotch, and only a quarter Cree. And I ain't got the blood of any tribe in my veins. Jest the same, Stevie is Métisse, and she'll tell you so with her head high."

"I know," Tam said. "I was teasing her, and I got a real lecture. She told me how the Bois Brûlés, the burntwood people, had blazed the long trails and hunted the plains in days before the whites dared their forts; how the Métis explored the passes and found the rich valleys. And how all they won is being taken from them."

"It's a bad thing," Devoe said. "Stevie is edicated; she thinks the claims and the petitions the Métis have sent to Ottawa will bring 'em their rights. She says the law will bring them justice. She's right, o' course, about how to do it. But Macdonald—Old Tomorrow, the Injuns call him—he ain't givin' in easy. I'm guessin' the Canadian Métis will get what the little boy shot at."

"It's hard for me to figure out the rights and wrongs of it," Tam said. "When Stephanie explained the proposed method of surveying the Métis' lands, it seemed like an outright steal to me. Stephanie puts great store by action in Ottawa, but I have to remember that in Manitoba the government promises did not stand."

"The whole thing is dynamite on a dam' short fuse," Devoe said. "Bad enough already, and now somebody is stirrin' up the

Métis on both sides of the border. Since most of 'em have dual citizenship, the border don't mean much to 'em."

"Do their leaders want trouble?" Tam asked.

"Hard to say. Pierre LaCroix is their governor in this section, and the Métis look up to him next to Louis Riel hisself. If somebody is gettin' to LaCroix, he's enough of a dreamer to risk big trouble. And a lot of fine lads would get theirselves killed, without a chance in God's green earth to win out."

"But with the government far away in Ottawa, and no railroad…"

"That's likely the carrot bein' held out to the Métis leaders," Devoe said. "The Dominion ain't a force to be discounted, Tam. Nor the Mounted Police. And back of them, there's that little lady of Windsor. She ain't in the habit of lettin' upstarts mess around with *her* Empire. No, it would take plenty of help from this side of the line for the Métis to claw out a foothold fer themselves along the Saskatchewan and the Belly."

"Who'd have the raw nerve for a filibuster?"

"Raw nerve—and plenty of money. I dunno, Tam. Not the Fenians; they ain't meant a thing since '71, when they turned tail at Pembina."

"Colly," Tam said, "I saw Cleland Strike meet your man LaCroix on the levee. They seemed friendly."

"And Strike has your money," Colly Devoe said thoughtfully. "It mought be, Tam; it mought be."

They were silent as they turned away from the river to the glade where the Devoe cabin stood in leafy shade.

That night a storm front bellied in, twisting mares'-tails of cloud spinning down the gray sky. They thickened and dropped an intermittent heavy drizzle over the land. On the hillside above the Métis camp, Tam and Stephanie stood looking down. When Tam had grown restless in the confines of the cabin, Stephanie had suggested a walk. Now Tam wondered if he had been wise in accepting, for his trouser legs were soaked to the knee.

"The Métis are sunny people. They hate the rain," Stephanie said.

The camp of the Bois Brûlés did look sad and forlorn under the gray skies. The camp was larger than Tam had thought. Its lodges were wet and bedraggled, the smoke from the vent flaps whipping flat down the wind. At the center was the brown Sibley of Pierre LaCroix, which doubled as a council tent. Its canvas was streaked with rain. Nothing moved in the drizzle; even the ubiquitous camp dogs had found shelter somewhere in the brush.

Tam glanced at Stephanie. Air and exercise had brought rich color to her lovely face. She had a thin wool shawl over her dark hair, and around her shoulders a Hudson's Bay blanket, draped serape fashion. Her beauty startled him. As if aware of his mood, she turned and led the way higher up the hill.

Here a rock ledge made an eave over a niche in the hill, too shallow to be called a cave, but dry under the overhang. Stephanie inspected the niche for possible rattlesnakes, then sat down on the shelf of stone. She motioned Tam to a place beside her. It was pleasant here, out of the rain but with the clean dampness still in their nostrils. Beyond, Tam saw the winding sweep of the Missouri, today surly and black as it raced along. Across the river the land drifted away into the low clouds, neither the Bearpaws nor the Highwoods visible in the creeping mist.

"We Scots have a contrary dourness," Tam said, gesturing toward the weeping land below. "So I rather like this weather. But I can see how people of French descent like the Métis might be depressed by it."

"They are," the girl said. "My people like to sing and dance and drink, with great gusto, with much noise and excitement. Ah, they do love gay times, and they hate bad weather, poor hunting, sickness, all the dull and routine things of life. On days like today," she said, laughing a little, "the burntwood people are not good companions."

"You're the exception, then," he said. "Stephanie, from the little I have seen of the Bois Brûlés, I find them both interesting and likable. They're a fine people, loyal, generous, deeply religious. I'm picking up a little of the language. Will you help me?"

"Of course. But since you already speak French, you won't find it difficult. It's based on old Norman French, changed by years and distance. And it's interspersed with Cree and Chippewa words, leavened by some English, even a little German. You'll soon be able to understand it, and be understood."

"I've got to do something," Tam said, frowning. "I'm certainly accomplishing nothing of what I was sent to Montana Territory to do. And it looks unlikely that I ever will."

"Don't be downcast, Tam," Stephanie said with quick sympathy. "The sway of Cleland Strike cannot last long. It must not."

"Meantime, though, what of the bank's money? Where shall I tell them it's going, if not into the cattle business?"

"For trouble and for death," she said strangely. "Oh, Tam, be patient. Don't challenge that man now. Time is with you. You will succeed. Tam, last night I lit a candle for you at my little shrine of St. Anne." She looked at him, a faint flush in the golden tan of her cheeks.

"Thank you, Stephanie," he said, touched by her faith.

"For the Métis, prayer is one of the few courses left," she said, staring toward the leaden clouds to the east. "God grant that they do not take any other. They have suffered much injustice, Tam. We—they found the waterways, the passes, the trails across the emptiness of the prairies. All this was our country, to roam and to live in. It fed us and we respected it.

"Then, in 1869, when the Hudson's Bay Company sold its tremendous lands to the Dominion, our people were left in the cold, not even consulted. The terms were considered outrageous by many of the winterers of the company itself. Then even before the Queen had signed the proclamation, rabid Canadians were swarming over the Métis lands, taking from us by force what my people had won by their pioneering, and in some cases by their very blood. Our land titles were declared worthless. We were to have no part in the formation of the new province."

She raised her head proudly. "Then we stood up with our rifles in our hands. Under the great Louis Riel, we forced the formation of the Province of Manitoba. The Dominion agreed to our proper representation, to our land rights, to an amnesty for all who had taken up arms. And we believed them. We disbanded quietly."

"The promises were not kept?" Tam asked.

"Of six hundred appointive offices in the new province, just five went to Métis," she said bitterly. "The new survey system, which the Dominion still insists upon, is making the land titles of the Canadian Métis worthless. We pile petition upon petition in Ottawa, but the Métis lands north of the border will fall to armed claim jumpers, unless John Macdonald listens to us."

"And the amnesty?"

Her hands went out in a helpless gesture. "Empty words. All the Métis governors, Riel, Nault, Lajimodiere, Delorme, Father Ritchot, Pierre LaCroix—they hunted them down like wild beasts. Many, having dual citizenship, escaped to the American side. They ran for their very lives after a drumhead court called the execution of Scott at Fort Garry outright murder. It wasn't, but the fiction served to keep our Louis Riel, duly elected to Parliament, from being seated. He too hurried across the line. He is in Montana now, an embittered man."

"Have the Métis no recourse?" Tam asked.

For a moment in her proud anger she looked all Indian.

"None," she said. "We are standing in the way of manifest destiny, even as the Sioux did, and the Blackfeet. North of the border, the government of Sir John Macdonald is driving as hard westward. My people are in the way. They could be crushed."

"But you are an American, Stephanie," he said.

"And I am proud of that, too, as many of my people are. But an imaginary line drawn across a wilderness can't keep a people from being one, Tam. We are joined by tradition and blood and legend. We want justice done. Is there no justice?"

In her voice was the deep hurt of betrayal. Whatever the rights of this thing, Tam thought, this girl is sincere. Choosing his words with care, he asked, "Stephanie, it will not come again to armed insurrection by the Métis?"

She gave him a strange look. "The good God knows we are nearly at the end of our rope, with nothing from Ottawa but delay and equivocation. So some of the more fiery spirits are arguing that since force won for us in Manitoba, why not in the Saskatchewan? This time, they say, we would be wiser. We would not let the fruits of victory be torn from us."

"And what do you think, Stevie?"

"I think it would be the worst mistake the Métis could make. Force breeds force, warping judgment, breeding reprisals. And my simple people have no idea of the stupendous and overwhelming strength that can and would be mustered against them. But I find it hard to discourage, Tam, when this empty game with Ottawa goes on and on, without satisfaction, without justice. The buffalo are nearly gone. My people ask, 'Can we eat petitions when we cannot hunt, and our lands are taken from us?'"

Tam had no answer. They sat silent, the rain dripping musically from the ledge in front of them, the wet landscape static in its aura of drifting cloud. The girl shivered, and Tam put his arm around her shoulders, drawing her to him. She did not resist, but let her head incline on his shoulder. He could smell the faint perfume of her hair, the wood smoke that clung to her garments, the flat odor of the wet wool of her blanket.

She said softly: "Tam, I'm frightened for my people. To be a success, a rebellion needs four things—men, money, arms, and bold leadership. All these things are being promised to the Métis.

And even with them, this rebellion would fail, against the might of the Dominion and the Empire."

"Who offers them this? Cleland Strike?"

"I think so. Women have small standing in the councils of the Métis, but I have heard things. Tam, heaven help the Bois Brûlés if they ever come under the domination of Clee Strike."

"But what would he gain? What's in it for him?"

"You've never seen it, Tam. But it is wide, rich country. Raw and formless now, but it holds furs and gold and land. The man behind the throne in the Northwest Territories could reap a vast fortune, if he were cunning and ruthless enough. And Cleland Strike is all of that."

"I agree. You hate him, Stephanie."

"Once I loved him. Tam, you must know this—I was coming back from St. Louis by steamer after my schooling. Clee Strike was aboard. He flattered me with his attentions, and by the time we reached Fort Benton I had promised to marry him."

"Damn him! To hoodwink an innocent child."

"I don't know how innocent, Tam. I had acquired fine airs during my schooling in the big city. It was like a romantic novel to have this fine gentleman wooing the little Métisse girl from the backwoods. When Clee wanted a quick wedding, I was even too happy with the situation to agree. I delayed."

"Something must have warned you."

She shook her head. "Good luck, more than good sense. Clee wanted a minister to marry us. But I was strong in the Faith. Then he argued for a prairie wedding, which the Church does permit if it is blessed by the priest at the first opportunity. Again I refused, for I had secret knowledge that Father Imoda was coming soon on his long and arduous circuit. When he arrived from St. Peter's Mission, I rushed to tell him my plans. At Clee Strike's name, he said: 'My daughter, this man—I married him last winter to a Cree woman, Maria Easy Walker. You cannot marry him.' "

"What did Strike say?"

"He was wild. He swore the good father lied. He said the woman was dead. And if she were not dead she was just a squaw. Her marriage to a white man meant nothing. I was crushed and sick. I gave him back his ring but I gave him one last chance. 'If the records at St. Peter's do not hold your name, I'll marry you,' I told him."

"The record was there, since you are not married."

She drew a chain from about her throat. She sprang its large heart-shaped locket open with a thumbnail. She took a tightly folded piece of paper from it and gave it to Tam:

*Die VC Marii 1878 Ego C. Imoda S.J. in missione St. Petri coram inhibito consensum pervabade praesenti solemniter matrimonio conjuncsi Cleland Johannum Strike filiam Grandison et Esther Strike Et Maria Easy Walker filiam Tom Easy Walker et Lily Eagle. Tests fuerunt Edward La Belle et Benjamin Ouellette.*

"This is an exact copy?" Tam asked.

She nodded. He handed it back to her. "The Latin limps in spots, but as your father might say, it's by bell, book, and candle."

"I'm past being sorry for myself," Stephanie said. "But I feel sad for the little Cree girl, with her baby."

"And this is the man Dove thinks she is married to," Tam said.

"I don't know this Dove. But may God help her, too, if she is tied to Cleland Strike," Stephanie said softly.

CLELAND STRIKE walked into the bunkhouse behind the house, straight from a meeting with Pierre LaCroix, Gabriel Valier, and some of the lesser Métis leaders. It had left Strike with the expansive feeling of euphoria that comes with power. He had made up all the ground lost for him the other day by that little idiot Dove (remember that, Clee, he told himself) by dint of minor concessions and a few specious statements. The planning thereafter had gone his way without a hitch. Now he was exultant, confident, loaded for bear.

"Where's Lisbon?" He asked the hostler, Kilgore, who was mending a harness strap in the fading light of a window.

"Backhouse. He'll be along," the old Irishman said, not looking up from his work. Strike stared at the man, frowning his displeasure.

"Any more come in today?" Strike asked.

"Twelve. Four by stage, five on horses borrowed or stole, three on shank's mare. Lisbon sent 'em on north in the mud wagon. The horses—and dam' poor nags they was—are at Perky's."

Strike rubbed his palms. "Good," he said. "How'd the men look?"

The Irishman gave him a shrewd look, narrowing his rheumy old eyes. "Ragtag and bobtail, mostly. One good man, mebbe two, out of the bunch. Christ, Strike, you can't depend on these saddle bums and ex-cons! Sure, they're mean and hungry enough to fight, but they just as lief fight each other. I'll lay a bet, once the wrinkles is out of their bellies, come trouble they'll scatter in all directions in a cloud of dust."

"You old fool, keep your silly opinions to yourself," Strike said sharply. "They'll fight for me. I know what I'm doing. Things are shaping up my way now."

"You got the Bois Brûlés where you want 'em?" Kilgore asked slyly.

The jab annoyed Strike. I'll get rid of this old troublemaker, he thought, if it is the last thing I do.

"I've had about enough of your smart-aleck insolence, old man," he said. "You tend to your own knitting or you'll land back in the gutter where I found you."

Kilgore did not answer, turning back to his work. Lisbon Frank came back into the bunkhouse.

"Where's Aleff?" Strike demanded.

The Portuguese wiped the back of his hand across his lips. "Out getting a snootful, I guess. He'll be along."

Consuming anger flared in Strike. "Booze and women, that's all the two of you think about," he said. "I'm getting sick of both of you. Hell, you've got the greatest chance you'll ever have in your lives, and you can't even stay sober. Dogs, and worse than dogs. At least a dog is true to his meat. I'd give half of what I own for a man I could trust—or a woman."

He gave the wooden bench a kick, upsetting the water bucket in a jangle of metal. He towered over the Portuguese, jabbing his index finger under the man's nose.

"Lisbon, you'd better get this. You bungled the last job I gave you, you and Aleff and Dirty Nose. That fool Smith paid with his life—not that it matters a rip to me, the damned bungler. The job wasn't done." He locked a powerful hand in the man's shirt front, wrenching him up on tiptoe. "You misbegotten mongrel, I'm only going to say this once: I want Thomas Barrie dead. I want Colly Devoe dead. And I want them dead soon. More than that, I want the life let out of Clip O'Boyle before the sun sets on next Sunday. You hear me?"

He thrust the man away from him. Lisbon Frank reeled against the wall. Strike pulled a handkerchief from his pocket and wiped his hands.

"But none of 'em is in Benton, Boss," the Portuguese whined. "We been lookin' for 'em."

"Fine Pinkertons you are—I was in the Métis camp less than an hour when one of the 'breeds slipped me the word. Barrie and Devoe are at Devoe's cabin, by the river beyond the Métis camp. The Fenian is lying low at Tuckatoose's squaw's cabin, hard by the portage upriver. So you know. Now I'm giving you five days, Lisbon. That's three days more than you ought to need. Then if the job isn't done, and done right, you and Aleff are for it. I'll call in Bryce Flinn and some other new scavengers, and put you two on the list."

Lisbon Frank started to protest. Strike shook a knotted fist. "Shut up!" he said. "Get that ape Aleff sobered up. Look to your horses. That O'Boyle is talking loud enough to be heard in Fort Macleod, and I want him silenced. Then take care of Barrie and Devoe. By Sunday night, Frank. You miss and you're dead!"

Contemptuously, he turned away. God, he thought, what imperfect tools a man has to contend with, when there's an empire at stake! But they're the only tools at hand, and I can't wait. The factors that are coming into conjunction will never exist simultaneously again. It will still be a bold and desperate gamble, but I've always loved the long chance. I've got to make my move before the new trans-Canada railroad gets across the pre-Cambrian Shield. I've got to move while old Tantanka Yatanka, Sitting Bull, is a threat like a drawn sword across the border. I've got to move before the temper of the Métis, which I've honed sharp, grows cold, or they get some redress for their wrongs. All things will be at a peak in a few weeks. My fighting men are nearly all in ....

Deep in thought, he walked toward the lights of the big house. He fumbled in his memory for words half forgotten, words that might have been written expressly for his enterprise. How did they go? *There is a tide in the affairs of men, which, taken at the flood, leads on to fortune…*

He could feel the swelling of that tide. He would turn it, by God, to his own account. In him rose a restless hunger, and, responding to the urgency, he looked up at the lighted window of their bedroom. He hurried into the house, his boots ringing sharp and hard on the polished floor. He flung off his coat and thrust open the door where Dove lay reading in the opal-globed lamplight.

"Brock got hisself in a jam, I know it," Colly Devoe said, shaking his head. "And it's my fault…."

"Papa, he's riding in now," Stephanie said. They went out on the porch in the gray dawn light, as the little man rode up.

He was toting a skinful. He was mud-spattered and whiskery, and he lurched when he slid down from his horse. He made a frantic grab to save the bottle that was tipping from his pocket. He wobbled to the porch step and sat down, with a long sigh. Thrusting his booted feet straight out before him, he uncorked the bottle.

"Have a snort, boys? Then the more fer me!" He sagged the level of the whisky in the bottle by a good inch. He leered at Devoe. "You think I got drunk a-purpose, Colly."

"Mebbe so, mebbe not," Devoe said, not critical. "Easy enough to get taken by the drink without intending. But Brock, I know you. Drunk or sober, you got the word you went after."

"In a manner of sp—speakin'," the solid man said with immense dignity, "You might say I have done so."

"You got it from the horse's mouth?" Colly asked.

"In a manner of sp—speakin', no," Brock said with another leer. "More like t'other … but fergit it. Man or booze was talkin'. The man was Clip O'Boyle."

"The Fenian? Hell, Brock, he ain't reliable. Clip's been battlin' John Barleycorn since Gettysburg, and he ain't won yet."

"'S'funny thing, though. Clip was sober when me'n' him started on the bottle before this yere one. Some of the truth leaked out of him, Col, I'll swear. Y'ought to talk to him."

"What did you learn?" Tam asked.

Brock shook his head owlishly. "You won't believe it, boys, lessen you git it from old Clip hisself. And you better be quick. The way ole Clip is talkin', somebody's gonna let the life out of him, and that sudden."

"Where can we find him?" Colly asked.

"He's holed up in the cabin of Tuckatoose's woman, about a mile beyant the big portage." Brock set the bottle beside him and leaned forward, his head in his hands. In a muffled voice he said, "Better ride out. Now."

"We will. But what's Clip got to say that's so all-fired important?"

Brock scrubbed hard at his cheeks with his palms, trying to fight off the whisky fumes. "A lot—lotta things. Can't 'member 'em. Mosht important one—Clee Strike, he's gonna be king of Northwest."

"Cattle king, you mean?" Tam asked.

"Hell, no! Real king, Clip said. One of them fellers sits around with gold jewelry on his head and a club in his hand, givin' orders. That kind. King Cleland the First, maybe."

"Brock, did he say ..." Tam began excitedly.

But Brock was through. His bleary eyes closed. Slowly, like a sawdust doll, he crumpled sideways on the porch. Gently, Devoe lifted the little man's feet and laid Brock straight on the boards. He placed the bottle of whisky within Brock's reach and straightened up.

"Tam, let's ride," he said. He pointed Indian fashion with a thrust of his chin at the sleeping Brock. He said to Stephanie:

"Take care of him, honey. An' don't stray more'n a foot from that Winchester until we git back. There's trouble in the wind."

"I can feel it," the girl said simply. "But you're riding toward it. Papa, be careful." She gave her father a quick hug. Then she looked at Tam, faint color rising in her cheeks. "And—and you, Tam, I don't want you hurt, either."

"Thanks, Stevie," Tam said, smiling. "Don't worry about me. I've always been an arrant coward. I fight shy of trouble."

"You a coward?" There was surprise in her voice.

"Always have been," he said cheerfully. "Scared of my own shadow. I look before I leap, run before I fight."

"Like hell," Colly Devoe said. "Now quit the lallygaggin', you two. Come on, Tam. Stevie, don't expect us until you see us."

They rode north along the river, rather than south toward the town. Urging his horse into the stream, Colly forced him through the shallows into the main current. Tam followed on his sorrel. He found the horse had to swim only a few yards, the river beginning to drop rapidly. On the far side they turned southeast, on a narrow trail muddy from rain. It led up out of the Missouri bottom into the morning sun, the horses steaming as they reached the tableland.

Across the river and away, they could catch a glimpse of the town. Colly put his horse to a canter, and Tam followed. Ahead the Highwoods loomed massive and touchable in the clean washed air. Far to the right, across furrowed breaks, Tam could see the peaks of the Little Belts and the low notch of Judith Gap. A big country, he thought for the hundredth time. It ought to be big enough for everyone to live without hate or bitterness or greed. But even here there was the same injustice, the same inhumanity that existed wherever men gathered together.

An odd thing, Tam thought, that a self-satisfied young banker should be drawn into this circle of hate and fear. The chain started by the arrival of Cleland Strike in Philadelphia was adding links to entangle Tam deeper. The shadow of Clee Strike seemed as inevitable as Nemesis herself. The man poisoned everything he touched. Everywhere, he left wreckage in his wake—a bigamous marrige to Dove, an abandoned lawful wife and child, and Stephanie Devoe, left scarred of heart and pride. He swore softly to himself.

"What kind of man is Cleland Strike, Colly?" he asked directly. "Does he think he is above all laws of man or God?"

"Clee Strike is an original, Tam. Ye cain't measure him by ordinary yardsticks. With women, with money, with men, he makes his own laws."

"How long will he get away with it?"

Devoe shook his head. "Hard to tell, Tam. Mebbe forever. I've learned that now and then a feller comes along that is outsize. Everything he does is a leetle bigger'n life. It may be good, it may be bad. But it's always got a breadth and a daring to it that takes the breath of ordinary mortals. Clee Strike is one sech— he's smart and tough and—and big, no matter how you size it up. It so happens he turned to the crooked way, so he's twict as crooked as most. They stop at murder, most of 'em. Strike, he stops at nothing." He was silent for a minute, looking off toward the blue-hazed horizon. "Tam, if that man had gone the right way, why, no tellin' where he might have ended up. But he didn't. He's bad, plumb bad. Tam, I like you. I'd hate to see it. But if it ever so happens you tangle head-on with Clee Strike, I'm afeerd fer ye."

Tam had lived with the same fear for months. He did not discount Devoe's warning. But he was human enough, and young enough, to resent Colly's low estimate of his abilities. A true estimate—for he had felt this untamed savagery in Strike, had suffered the brutal punishment of the man's fists. He shivered now in the hot sunshine, remembering the pain and the hurt of the beating, the humiliation of being beaten with Dove standing by, her hands pressed against her mouth. Dove had egged him on to

take her to a dancing party, in spite of Strike's cold warnings to
both of them. She had played one against the other in the age-old
game of the coquette. But it was Tam who got hurt. Not Dove.

In the flood of self-reproach for his own inadequacy, Tam
dropped back, to be alone with his bitter thoughts. The sun
climbed higher in the brassy bowl of the sky. Tam hardly watched
where they were going.

Colly Devoe reined in his horse on a hilltop. He pointed
down.

"Tuckatoose's woman lives in the next coulee," he said. "Best
if we come on the cabin gradual. Clip O'Boyle is likely loaded fer
bear, and nervous to boot. Keep your eyes open."

They rode down a steep, slippery trail. Up the coulee, the
weathered logs of the cabin blended into the gray clay of the hillside. They stopped at long rifle range, and Colly Devoe gave an
odd whistle. Tam saw the door open just a crack. It stayed that
way for some time, then opened. A hand beckoned.

They rode up to the cabin, tied their horses, and went to the
door. "Come in! Come in!" a bull voice roared. Tam followed
Colly inside.

The solid stink of the place nearly gagged him. And Colly
too, for he said "Clip, the air in this place would strangle a mink.
Don't you ever wash?"

"Naw. I like bein' dirty," the burly man said. He was sprawled
across the tangled bed. He wore neither shirt nor trousers, his
long drawers and knit singlet so dirty they might have been dyed
black. He sat up, shaking his head, rubbing his bloodshot eyes.
He gave a prodigious yawn and scratched at his belly with both
hands, like a huge and mangy ape.

"Where's the woman?" Devoe asked.

"Kicked her out, the fool," O'Boyle said.

Tam studied the man. He had learned that O'Boyle had come
west with General Donnell after the ill-starred Pembina Raid in
1871, the final foray of the Fenian movement. While the Irish still

talked big, and Donnell waved the Fenian flag on safe occasions, he was a respectable lawyer now, and careful not to jeopardize his community standing. This Clip O'Boyle was so busy drinking himself to death that manifest destiny was now an empty phrase. All the old Fenians would argue in barrooms the still widely held proposition that the Northwest Territories should be part of the United States. But as long as there was whisky, Clip O'Boyle would hardly bother his head about annexation. Nor would any other man in this day and age.

"I hear you have a fairy story for us," Devoe said.

O'Boyle glared. "I told Brock nothing."

"I'm asking you, not Brock."

"The back of me hand to the likes of ye, damn ye. Tryin' to put words in me mouth. Botherin' me when I'm tryin' to get me rest." He yawned again, showing snagged and yellow teeth. He leaned back and shut his eyes.

Colly winked at Tam. He took a quart bottle of whisky from his pocket and pulled the cork with his teeth. Reaching over, he waved the neck of it under the Irishman's carbuncle of a nose. O'Boyle's bleared eyes snapped open. He came up on one elbow, the other hand swooping around to snatch the bottle. He tipped it up, the liquor dribbling from the corners of his mouth. At last he lowered it, took a deep breath, and wiped his lips with the back of his hand.

"Oh, foine stuff, foine. And foine fellers ye are, if 'tis fer me."

"You put the dent in it, it's yours," Colly said. "And another like it in Tam's coat pocket."

O'Boyle scowled. He held the bottle off at arm's length. He squinted at it, then took another stout draught. Clutching the bottle close to his chest, he said "So they're mine if I talk. Then talk I will, though it seals me death warrant, for I do love the crayture beyond anythin' that's left to me in life. I'll talk. But let me have one small dram more, in case me throat gets dry."

He took a long pull and set the bottle on the table, within reach. "Now, where should I start?"

"Is Strike stirring up the Métis?" Tam asked. "What devil's brew is boiling along the Whoop-Up? What does Strike aim to do?"

"Lad, ye come to the right man fer the answers, though I get meself kilt fer the tellin'. Boys, this summer the country is a powder keg, the Métis achin' with their wrongs, Sittin' Bull squattin' jest acrost the border like an auld timber wolf; the buffalo about gone, the Injuns worritin' about meat fer their families; the Mounties and the troops alike pyrootin' around the countryside; the traders cuttin' each other's throats, the politicians raisn' hob and cheatin' honest men—ah, lads, there's trouble along the border. Gin'ral Donnell, the auld fool, he's still oratin' that manifest destiny points north. That same, I say, is a dom' lie. To hell with manifest destiny, when all of us in the Whoop-Up is sittin' on a powder kag. And who will light the fuse?"

"Clee Strike?" Colly asked.

"None other. He stirs up here, he bribes over yon, he cuts a throat here and there where it will do him the most good. Big promises he makes to the Métis, bull-con he hands to the Army. And the while he's gatherin' in the hardcases fer his own privit army. He's going to cut up a fat hog, that Strike."

"And for what purpose, O'Boyle?" Tam asked.

The Irishman leaned forward. "He aims to take over that whole country north of the Line, as far east as he dares. He would set up the Métis as a new nation, and himself king of it." He took a belt at the bottle. "King Cleland the First! And, boys, likely the Last."

"Don't think that omadhaun is crazy, Colly," O'Boyle said, shaking a dirty finger at him. "I misdoubt he kin win. But if anybody kin come close to twistin' the lion's tail and rufflin' the eagle's feathers at the same time, it's this same Clee Strike."

# 8

"WHERE DID you learn all this, Clip?" Colly asked bluntly.
"I was an undercover man for Gin'ral Donnell,
recruitin' Army deserters, and Mountie deserters, wolfers
and renegades and auld sojers down on their luck. He tells me
any hardnose lad with blood in his eye is me meat fer Strike's
privit army. I even made a trip to Oregon on the business.
Then Donnell, the auld fool, got the idea he was runnin' the
show. First thing I know, Strike has tossed me and the gin'ral
right out of a job on our behinds. He warned Donnell: 'You
squeak, no more law business from me ner the bank." With
me, it was a dom' sight simpler." He dragged at the bottle,
nearly empty now.

"How is that, Clip?" Tam asked.

"He passed the word he wanted me hide nailed to the wall.
I got out of town between days. Though he'll git me yet, for the
man is a divil. You see why I must keep up me courage."

"Sure, Clip, sure," Colly said. "Where is this training ground
of Strike's located?"

O'Boyle sagged back in the rats'-nest of a bed. "Up around
the Three Buttes somewhere. Stay away from it, or ye'll get your
gizzards slit. Now go away. Give me me other bottle, and leave
me to drown me sorrows and me fears."

Colly nodded to Tam. Tam took the second bottle from his
pocket and put it on the table. They walked out into the hot wash
of the sunshine, the fine freshness of the air. As they untied their
horses, they heard O'Boyle muttering in the cabin.

Tam swung into the saddle. His horse shied at something. Tam leaned forward to quiet it. And the slam of a rifle came from above on the ridge. Lead chugged into the log wall of the cabin.

"Ride, Tam!" Colly Devoe shouted. Tam jammed spurs into his horse, and the animal surged in a great leap along the coulee trail. Then they were safe under the slope of the bank. They reined in and looked back, Colly drawing his six-shooter.

They saw the door of the cabin swing open. Clip O'Boyle came staggering out in his dirty underwear. He was clutching the bottle to his chest. A rifle slammed, and the bottle blew apart in a flare of shining shards. The heavy slug flung O'Boyle back against the cabin wall. His knees buckled and he slid down. He pitched forward at the last, to lie motionless. Then his body jumped as the hidden rifleman drove two, three, four unnecessary bullets into the corpse.

Tam swallowed, sick. Devoe swore bitterly. He motioned to Tam and they spurred their horses up the trail.

"We cain't do a thing fer Clip," Colly said. "But we kin save our own hides. Let's git out before they flank us."

The rifles had fired from the Fort Benton side. So they turned south and west, into the long breaks, caring little for direction, concentrating on distance. Several miles of broken country lay behind them when Colly pulled his tired horse to a halt on the top of a ridge. Tam reined up beside him.

Their back trail lay empty. But far back, where the river glistened at a bend, a thin haze of blue smoke plumed up and away on the wind. That would be the pyre of Clip O'Boyle, Tam knew. The killers had put the torch to the cabin of Tuckatoose's woman.

Tam leaned forward, palms on the saddle horn. "The devils! That was close, Colly. How much truth did O'Boyle talk?"

"One part Irish brag, three, four parts truth, I'd jedge. What he said fits. Explains why Pierre LaCroix is so thick with Strike. LaCroix is an ambitious man, though he is truly on the side of the Métis. I'll bet Pierre thinks he is outsmarting Clee Strike, using him fer his own ends. Tam, if he is he'll be almighty sorry. Strike's too big fer him."

"And too ruthless. O'Boyle must have been on the inside, or he wouldn't have been gunned down. Nor did they aim to let us get away, either." He shivered a little. "Wonder who they were?"

"A couple of Strike's bully boys," Colly said. "Maybe Lisbon Frank and another. Lucky the one who was using the .45-70 was such a pox-poor shot. That miss warned us. The other, the one that pumped the exter .44-40 slugs into pore Clip, he would have shot us inter doll rags, given a second or two. He kin shoot."

Tam shook his head. "Colly, I've been scared to death from the day I came into Montana Territory. I'm getting more scared by the minute. But scared or not, this plan of Strike's must be broken up. The Métis can't stand up against the armed might of the British Empire for long, and that's what it would come to, sooner or later. I don't care about Pierre LaCroix, but I like these burntwood people. I would hate to see these good men die trying to make good Strike's crazy dreams of empire."

"I'm with ye," Devoe said, spitting into the parched earth. "But you tell me how to stop it."

"The sheriff? The U.S. Marshal?"

"They are good men, and brave. But Strike has enough men to eat both of 'em alive, together with any posse they might gather,"

"That leaves the Army."

Colly Devoe frowned. "You ever dealt with the Army, Tam? Clee Strike could git to be king of Canady and Borneo and Timbuktu, by the time the Army got done sendin' telegrams to Fort Keogh and Fort Snelling and Wash'n'ton and all the way back again, tryin' to git a little live ammunition to shoot at the renegades. Tam, if Sittin' Bull ever busts back acrost the border and his braves cut them telegrapht wires, the Army will bog down like a freight hitch in quicksand."

"Still, it looks like our only chance," Tam said. "I'd like to talk to the commanding officer at Fort Shaw."

"S'posen he was on Clee Strike's pay roll?"

Tam was aghast. "Would Strike dare bribe an Army officer?"

"Strike will dare anything. Them lads in blue is paid dam' poor, Tam. The life is hard, and advancement don't amount to shucks in the peacetime Army. And if this same man honestly believed the U.S. had a good claim to all the land from here plumb to Alasky, mebbe he wouldn't feel wrong to take money fer helpin' makin' it a fact."

"But we've got to try," Tam said stubbornly.

Colly Devoe shrugged. "All right. It's better'n forty mile from here to Fort Shaw. There's a ranch on Sun River where we kin sleep, and hit Shaw in the mornin'. But promise one thing, Tam. When you talk to this officer, don't blurt out the whole story. Kinda feel him out. Or we might be left with our tails in the gate."

"I'll agree to that," Tam said, for he respected the force of Colly's logic. "Let's go."

They made their way through the broken country along the south bank of the river over the faintest of trails. The coulees were deep, some of them almost canyons by the time they hit the river. It was well past noon when the two men came into a wider valley. They stopped for nooning by a large stream of clear, cold water.

"Belt Crick," Colly said. "Out of the mountains to the south."

From a saddlebag he took pemmican and ship's biscuit. There was little taste to the meal, but with the rest and a drink of the cold creek water, Tam felt much less weary when they mounted.

Out of the valley, they rode along a high bluff above the Missouri. Ahead a muted roar grew louder. When Colly rode to the edge of the bluff, Tam followed. Below, the river tumbled over a massive ledge of rock in a great cataract, the mist drifting from it down the gorge. Tam had seen Niagara, but he found this great fall almost as impressive.

Four other falls they saw in their westward course. Then the canyon grew less precipitous. The river curved in from the south through rolling prairie to the upper of the falls. Beyond the Missouri spread a wide green valley, with the silver cord of a smaller river twisting through it.

"Sun River," Colly said, pointing. "Joins the Big Muddy right there. We'll find a ford jest below, and cross."

They forded the Missouri about half a mile below its confluence with the Sun. Though wide and swift, the water did not come past the bellies of the horses. As they came dripping up the west bank, a herd of deer went bounding away into the underbrush.

They rode west into the harsh light of the setting sun. Several miles up the lush valley they came on a log house, with a pole corral and a clumsy barn. Colly gave a hail. From the cabin came a grizzled man, one hand on the butt of his pistol. Seeing Colly, he relaxed.

"Dog it, you old hoss stealer, ain't seed you fer a coon's age," he cried. "Light and set, boys. Jest in time fer supper."

"Sounds good," Colly said, swinging down. "Jem, meet my good friend Tam Barrie. We're bound fer Fort Shaw, but we'd as lief stop fer the night right here, if you don't mind."

"Sho', it would pleasure me," Jem said, grinning. "I jest come back from there, s'afternoon late."

The supper was tough beef, soggy sourdough bread, and coffee as muddy as a swamp and as bitter as gall. But Tam ate it and enjoyed it, remembering Colly's saying about the sauce of hunger. Afterward they tried to talk, but all of them, Jem included, were drugged by weariness. Jem struggled to keep his eyes open. Finally he said, "I got me an extry bed, room enough fer both."

"You still got that loft of prairie hay, Jem? Then me'n' Tam will bed down out there. They say more people die in bed than any other place, so we ain't takin' no chances!"

Jem guffawed and went to get a lantern.

When they were stretched out in the sweet hay of the loft, Colly said: "Jem's a fine feller. But them beds of his'n are so full of varmints they'll walk off by theirselves someday. I knowed there wa'n't no bedbugs in this hay."

Jest then there was a rustle in a corner of the loft. Tam raised up on an elbow. "What was that?" he asked.

"Mice, boy, mice," Colly said impatiently. "They won't eat ye. Git to sleep, daggone it."

A moment later Tam felt Colly shaking him. He wedged open his eyes. A thin beam of sunlight was streaming through a knothole in the roof. "Time to get up?" he mumbled.

"And long past," Colly said. He reached for his vest. "Come alive, son. Man has to be in topnotch condition to cope with Jem's flapjacks."

They walked to the house in the crisp bright sunlight. Jem had the batter mixed, and dished up his tough, filling flapjacks as long as the two would eat. On the side he had home-cured bacon, wild honey and, wonder of wonders, fresh eggs.

"One more stack, Colly?" Jem asked, at the big range.

"Well, it ain't safe, but shove 'em along," Colly said.

The stringy rancher came over with his own filled plate and his cup of inky coffee. "Say, what's so all-fired important over to Fort Shaw?" he asked. "Half o' Benton's been there."

Colly Devoe put down his fork. "Who, for instance?"

"Why, yestiddy, when I was deliverin' my garden truck, I seen Gin'ral Donnell ride in. A while later here come Clee Strike, ridin' hard. I was visitin' on Washboard Row when I ketched sight of the gin'ral ride out through the gate, his coattails claw-hammered inter the wind, that phiz of his lookin' like a spanked baby. Then, jest about when I headed back, I dang near run into the Portugee, Lisbon Frank, and that ape Con Aleff, ridin' fer the fort, hellbent fer leather."

"Had Strike gone by then?" Tam asked.

"Naw. As I went by the colonel's office I looked in the open window. There was Clee Strike as big as life, smokin' a big black stogie; and the colonel, he was laughin' at something' Strike had told him. Strike's hoss was still switch-in' flies at the rail when I rode out."

Colly said, "Well, that tears the rag off'n the bush."

"Guess we wasted a long ride," Tam agreed, disappointed and dully angry. The trader must have corrupted Army personnel, on the face of it. Now there was no remedy.

"Jem, we changed out minds," Colly told the rancher. "We're headin' straight across for Benton. But I'd like to borry the lend of that Winchester of yours. Send it back on the stage."

Jem reached up and took the rifle from its pegs.

"They say there's a varmit or two betwixt here and Benton," he said.

"Coyotes, mostly," Colly said, squinting along the sights. He thumbed shells into the receiver. "Or hydrophoby skunks."

"If they git too thick, Colly, jest remember this piece throws a mite high and to the left," Jem said, and leered knowingly.

There was a whine in Lisbon's voice. "I tell you, Clee, we done our damnedest."

Shifting in the saddle, Strike stared at the Portuguese. "You call it that?" he asked coldly. "The two of you lay around Benton for one whole day because of a little rain. The next, you let Barrie and Devoe get to Clip O'Boyle before you. Then, when you had the three of them under your sights, you missed. I'm even wondering if you killed O'Boyle."

"He's dead all right," Lisbon Frank said. "I got him four times, right in the brisket. I seen the dust jump out of his undershirt as the slugs took him."

"What happened to Barrie and Devoe?"

The Portuguese slid an uneasy glance toward Con Aleff. The surly giant said: "He give me first shot and I missed 'em clean. Dam' gun threw high, and they got out fast."

"Con, the truth—were you drunk two days ago?" Strike's voice was biting.

The big man scowled. Slowly he nodded.

"And the day before? And the day before that? And the only reason you weren't drunk yesterday was that Frank dragged you out of town before you had time to skirmish up a bottle?"

The big man was silent. He lowered his head.

"Let's have your pistol," Strike said. Aleff stared at him. then slowly unholstered it and handed it over. Strike tossed it to Lisbon Frank.

"Frank, ride ahead to the top of the rise," he said. "If anyone rides this way, signal with two quick shots. Con, come along with me."

Without waiting, he spurred his horse off the Benton road and into a coulee. Aleff hesitated, then rode after him. Lisbon Frank watched them out of sight, then rode to the top of the rise, and waited. He leaned forward tensely in the saddle, watching the road below, watching the mouth of the coulee. He jerked in the saddle as he heard the muffled slam of a single shot. When Cleland Strike came riding out of the defile alone, his face stone hard, the Portuguese manged to sit impassive, except for the flicker of a muscle that twitched in his scarred cheek.

Strike said: "The job is still yours to finish, Frank. I'll bring Bryce Flinn in from the ranch to side you. He'll do more for you than—" he made a quick gesture toward the coulee. "Get this, Frank. From this moment I want you and Bryce to track Devoe and Barrie down like a pair of wolves. They're dangerous—I want them dead. When you have disposed of them, you pick up that slut of a daughter of Devoe's."

"Stephanie? She's a handsome piece, that half-breed," Lisbon Frank said, licking dry lips. "We might have some fun..."

"You lay one finger on her, beyond what it takes to tie her, and I'll kill you dead, Frank. Bring her to me unharmed, you hear?"

"I hear you, Boss," the Portuguese said, his voice taut.

"All right. I'm heading north at sundown. Join me there. With the girl, and with the scalps of those two meddlers." He did not wait for an answer, but spurred over the ridge and northeast toward Fort Benton.

Strike walked into the kitchen of his house in the early twilight. Sophie Valier was working at the kitchen table, humming a tuneless little song. He stopped beside her, gave her terse orders. Her face showed a momentary surprise, then went carefully blank again. He went on into the parlor.

Dove was intent on a book, in the light of a student lamp. He stood in the doorway watching her. She seemed calm, but the lace fichu at her breast trembled a little to her breathing. Strike took two strides. Reaching down, he pinned her wrists with one hand with cruel force, and snatched her to her feet, the book tumbling to the rug. She cried out at the pain, her eyes frightened. He thrust his hand against the firm swell of her breast, to feel the racing of her heart.

"Why so frightened, Dove, my dear?" he asked.

"Clee you're hurting me! Let me go," she cried.

He thrust her back onto the sofa. He stood over her as she sat rubbing her chafed wrists.

"Dove, did you enjoy reading all my private papers?" he asked. "It wasn't wise of you, my dear, to have a key to my strongbox made by the same man who made the box for me. He told me about it."

Dove's hand went to her mouth. Her eyes were hunted. Then she mustered some bravado. "It looks as if no one is to be trusted, these days," she said.

"A truth to be learned early in life," he said. "Of course, I have never trusted you, my pretty. But I had to impress your father and his friends, to get the loan I had to have. And there is nothing that impresses more than a wedding."

"Then your love for me…"

"Is real enough, in spite of your treachery and your lying. Dove, I love that pretty face of yours, and that delectable body. I admire the sassy temper, and the mean stubborn streak in you. In my day, my dear, I was an expert horsebreaker. I enjoyed the work. But I'm sure I did not enjoy it half so much as I'll enjoy breaking you."

"You'll never break me, Clee Strike!" she flared. "You and your big talk—just like this mad gamble of yours."

"So you did read my papers."

"I read them. Clee, what you plan is insane beyond belief."

"No, it is cold fact, and I am going to succeed," he said without anger. "You have a part in this plan, Dove. I'll watch you with enjoyment, savoring the possibility that you may turn traitor—which means, very literally, that your pretty neck will be broken. Remember that, Dove."

"What part must I play?" she asked.

"I'm not going over the history of Canada in the last thirty years. Surely Miss Clevenger's School must have taught you something. But in that history the facts were there, for anyone to read. Your husband seems to be the only one who can read them, and to have sufficient audacity to take advantage. Several powerful forces will climax in this year of 1880, never to occur again. While they are here, I plan to use them to the hilt."

"They include LaCroix and the Métis?"

He nodded. "They form a part. Sitting Bull another, the lack of a railroad across the north edge of the continent another. My plan is simple—the Métis, to right the immense wrongs they have suffered under the Macdonald government, will rebel and form their own government, just as they did in Manitoba under Louis Riel. LaCroix will become governor. I will back the Métis with two hundred well-armed hardcase veterans of my own. We'll sweep the Mounted Police aside, and before the Dominion Government can move I'll have my own government-in-being solidly entrenched in the Northwest Territories. I'll demand recognition and aid from the United States, and I'll get them. And Ottawa will be tied in a strait jacket."

"And where do you reap your profit, Clee?" she asked.

"*Our* profit, my dear. Well, it will be glorious to be known as the man who carved out an empire. But more to the point, Cleland Strike and Company will be given tremendous concessions, in furs and transportation and mining, in water rights and good farm land. With Pierre LaCroix for a figurehead, I'll milk the Northwest dry. I'm putting plenty of money into this thing, but by God, I'll make it come back a thousandfold!"

She gave him an odd look. "What then of the rights of the Métis? What of the justice they will be fighting for?"

He laughed. "The Métis be damned! What of Cleland Strike and his beautiful wife? That's more to the point. Dove, once before a man stood on the pinnacle I'm climbing—Louis Riel. He held Manitoba in the palm of his hand, but he wasn't smart enough or ruthless enough to make his play stand. But, unlike Riel, I am the least sentimental of men. There are millions of dollars to be made in this affair, so God help anyone who stands in my way. You too, Dove. But play my game and you'll wear diamonds."

# 9

"GOVERNOR STRIKE," Dove said softly, as if trying the sound of it.

"Or prime minister, or even king, for that matter," he said. "But you can bet your life that where I am, there will the vultures gather. No one—you hear, Dove?—no one will stand against Cleland Strike, and live."

What she saw in his eyes dismayed her. She was visibly shaken. "Clee, can you challenge the armed might of two continents?"

"Certainly, when that might is so far from Whoop-Up country. Yesterday, rather slyly I thought, I sounded out our U.S. Army. They pose no threat, I'm sure. Especially if all the officers are like the colonel commanding at Fort Shaw. A blundering blowhard who can't spit without telegraphing Fort Snelling."

"But beyond the border?"

He waved a hand airily. "Before Ottawa can move against me, I'll either be firmly in the saddle or have LaCroix there. Either way, we'll best any army they can send against us. I'll parlay the bank's paltry thousands into millions."

"I'm afraid of it, Clee," she said. "For me and for yourself. You're brewing tragedy and death. And I know of one man who will oppose you."

"Tam Barrie, I suppose. Never mind him, Dove. He is under the interdict."

"You have ordered his death?" she asked, her voice shaken.

"Not Tam, Clee. Not poor helpless Tam. Send him home . . . ."

He shook his head. "No, Dove. Tam Barrie is a stinking little coward, but I need that money from his bank too badly to suffer even his slight threat toward it. It is the sinews of war. No, my hounds are on his scent. I'll feel much better when he's rotting at the bottom of some dry gulch back on the prairie."

She put her hands on his arms, looking up at him with tears in her eyes. "Clee, for my sake," she pleaded.

"The orders are out. He's as good as dead this minute," he said, a thin note of pleasure in his voice.

She stared at him, her eyes bleak, as if something had died within her. "Then I'll warn him," she said.

He pushed her back to the sofa. "Oh, no, sweetheart. You won't have time. You're going north with me—you have twenty minutes to pack one small trunk. Leave out the frills and the laces and the low-cut gowns; there will be nobody in camp to impress except me. And you can impress me in other ways."

"Why must I go?"

"Because I don't trust you out of my sight."

"I'll pack in the morning."

"You'll pack now," he said. "In twenty minutes. If you're not ready then, you're coming anyhow, even if you're stark naked. Make up your mind, Dove. I'm tired of your stubbornness."

Dove didn't wait. She picked up her skirts and ran for the stairs, making a little sobbing noise in her throat as she hurried.

Twenty minutes, or a very little longer—it was already pitch dark when Strike heaved the little trunk into the back of the buggy and lifted Dove into the seat. "Line out," he told the driver.

"Hoh!" the driver yelled, reaching out. The whiplash stung the rumps of the team and they sprang forward, for a moment tipping the buggy up on two wheels. Dove, with dismay and fear, recognized the driver as the Métisse woman, Sophie Valier. She shrank away from her into the corner of the seat, as the woman swung the team out of the gate. They were running hard over the hill to the northwest as Sophie straightened them out.

The woman has cat's eyes, Dove thought. I can't see the smallest sign of a road. The stars were winking in the clear air with a brillance she had never seen, the soft eerie glow of them falling across the prairie. The ground itself was smoky shadow, but the Métisse did not hesitate. She laid the lash across the backs of the horses. The buggy spun into the flat above the town with the four outriders galloping their horses to keep up.

When the horses had run the edge off their wildness and settled down to a steady trot, Dove relaxed a little. She saw the Métisse turn toward her.

"How you like dat?" Sophie asked, not unfriendly.

"Very exciting," Dove said. Timidly she added, "You drive very well, Sophie."

"Drive team since liddle girl," Sophie Valier said. "You think you like camp?"

"I don't know. Will there be any other ladies there?"

Sophie Valier laughed, full-throated, hearty. "Ladies? huh! Mebbe six women from Butte City, for entertain de men. Five Métisse, wash, cook, clean de clothes. Couple, three full-bloods, help Métisse. No ladies. Except you and me." She leaned toward Dove, her eyes lambent in the pale light. "You be good girl, get along fine. You act like bitch, you be sorry."

Dove shrank back in her corner. The very tone of the woman's voice made her uneasy. For this uneasiness she felt anger and contempt at herself. Dove Demarest had never been afraid to put her hunter at the stiffest jump, or to face man or woman on her own terms and win. But the terms were different now. She felt the fear mounting in little waves. It's bad, she thought. Is this how Tam felt when Clee was beating him down?

She edged away from the thought. "Sophie," she asked, "are there a great many men there? Will it be exciting?"

The woman grunted. "Many men, all right. Plenty excitement in five, six, seven days. We march across border. We fight for justice, maybe kill some of Mounties, maybe get some men killed ourselves. They kill us, we kill Canucks same tam, you bet."

"You believe in this raid, Sophie?" Dove asked, worried.

The woman hesitated a long time. Then she said: "My brother, he's friend Pierre LaCroix. He is worried, my brother. Me, I am worried too. I remember Louis Riel. Then I think maybe she is not so good for Bois Brûlés, this raid."

She touched up the horses, and the buggy reeled on into the silken night. Dove, huddled in her corner, dozed, opening her eyes now and then to stare at the silver carpet of the starlight. She wondered once where Tam might be, Tam under sentence of death. Remembering Tam, she remembered how she had scratched the surface of Cleland Strike, her husband, and under the civilized veneer found a man of stone and steel. She loved him. But she was wondering if the man she loved was the man she knew, or this stranger in the same flesh. She felt cold and naked, as if she were a child who had been forced to grow up all at once.

She shifted her position on the seat, trying to find some posture less painful than another. In misery and discomfort, she sagged to the racking motion, too beaten to rebel. At last her tortured body dropped into a fitful sleep.

With Strike's hounds ranging afar, Colly Devoe and Tam swung wide around Benton to the north. The way took them along the Teton bottoms, where they sweated in the moist heat and fought clouds of avid mosquitoes. Almost to the confluence of the Teton and the Marias, Colly turned east again. They crossed the steep ridge of the Crocon de Nez, the height of land that held the Teton away from the Missouri. They rode into camp without challenge, in the late afternoon.

"The Métis are gone," Stephanie said in greeting.

"To the north?" Tam asked.

She nodded, worry in her dark eyes. "I don't like it," she said. "Brock rode over and tried to question them. But he got nowhere."

The solid man said: "Some way they got word about mid-morning. Such a flurry and scurry you never did see. Took 'em only about a hour to pack up, lock, stock, and bar'l. They lit out, the kids hollerin', the dogs barkin', the dust as thick as smoke from a prairie fire. They strung out to the north like the Old Nick hisself was after 'em."

"You didn't see the messenger?" Colly asked.

Brock shook his head. "Could'a' been anybody. But he sure brought powerful medicine, whatever it was. You see Clip O'Boyle?"

"We saw him," Colly said grimly.

"He tell you anything?"

"Plenty. And not a minute too soon."

"So they got him, after all."

"Right at our backs. And dam' near drilled us too; didn't miss Tam by more'n the skin of his teeth. We taken out, headin' south, aimed to tell our troubles to the Army at Fort Shaw. But we stopped overnight with Jem, found out Strike had already been to the fort. Jem seen him bein' real chummy with the colonel in command. So no use of us spillin' our woes to that man. We turned around and came home."

"Papa, could Clee Strike bribe an Army officer?" Stephanie asked.

Tam answered for him. "He didn't have to, Stevie. All that was necessary was that he be on good terms with the man. No doubt, too, he has done favors for those people. Thus his word would carry much more weight than the word of a mule skinner or a bank clerk. We'd have tipped our hand, but gotten nowhere."

"Still, you might have tried..."

"Only time will tell, honey," Colly told her. "But we did learn that this business is comin' to a head soon. And there's nobody honin' to stop it except us."

"We must stop it, or there will be mourning in the homes of the Bois Brûlés," Stephanie said. "But how, Papa?"

"Well, it's a dead immortal cinch we ain't gonna stop it here in Benton. Stevie, you pack up the panniers with the camp kit and vittles for a week or two. We'll ride north at dawn."

Brock winced a little. "Colly, you know I cain't be depended on, after that bresh with the Gros Ventres in '73. I'm like to turn tail. You want me along?"

Colly laughed his great laugh, clapping the solid man on the shoulder. "You're about as scairt as the man that sticks his head in the lion's mouth at the circus. I know what ails ye, Brock. The sight of a scarlet tunic makes you queasy ever since that Cypress Hills business. Dunno as I blame ye. The Queen would still like to stretch a neck or two over that affair. So you might as well stay. Somebody ought to keep an eye on the place."

Brock grinned his relief and rode off to his own small cabin around the bend of the hill.

It was cool at dawn, but as they rode down the long morning the heat mounted, prickling the skin. Stephanie rode beside Tam, subdued and withdrawn. Then gradually color came to her cheeks and sparkle to her eyes. The day stirred Tam's blood too: bright and clear, the grass green-yellow along the benches, the willows gray-green in the bottoms. Now a soft sweet breeze sprang up, and the horses picked up their pace.

Tam looked admiringly at the girl. By now he was used to the way she rode astride, her fringed buckskin dress hiked up on her slim lovely legs, as the Indian women rode. He smiled to himself, picturing some of the imperious belles of Philadelphia riding Indian fashion. The comparison was not unfavorable to Stephanie. Admiring the loveliness of the girl's face and body, he turned the scales and wondered how she would look in a low-cut ball gown of white satin, her midnight hair coiffed stylishly high. He knew she would be sensational. Too bad, he thought, that she has Indian blood. And instantly was ashamed of himself.

With the two pack horses trailing, they splashed through the ford of the Teton at Captain Nelse's ranch. They pulled neckerchiefs up around their mouths as they crossed Yeast Powder Flat. Even then the dust sifted through, clogging nose and throat. Only when they reached the high ground on the far side could they beat the dust from their clothes, and hawk and spit until they could breathe again.

They took a short nooning at a cold spring. Then they pushed north in the heavy heat of the afternoon, plagued by flies and prickly pear and dust devils. They spoke little, enduring the discomfort in mutual misery, watching the small dramas of the prairie. Once a small herd of deer erupted from a spring thicket, a gray coyote trotting after them, waiting his chance. Colly reached for his pistol, but the beast slid away like a gray ghost and was gone. A hawk stooped from the blue into the sage, and flapped heavily skyward again, something kicking in his cruel talons.

In the hypnotic discomfort of the ride, Tam found himself lost in far thoughts. He thought of home, cold and precise, with little love within its walls. It surprised him now that of his childhood, the only pleasant days he remembered were the visits to his distant cousin, Dove Demarest, in the great house set amid its spacious lawns. Dove had been, then as now, headstrong, impulsive, and lovely. Ah, but she had queened it over him. Dove Strike, she was called now. For who would tell her of a copper-skinned girl child named Maria Easy Walker? Not Tam Barrie.

He could see the sawtoothed rampart low in the west that was the main range of the Rockies, when Colly turned his horse north along the valley of the Marias. They came to a small creek screened by willow and alder. Colly rode through a gap in the undergrowth, followed by Tam and Stephanie, with the pack horses. They broke into a pleasant glade, where the spring-fed creek widened into a substantial pond, the margins lush with grass. It was shaded by a hill, shielded from the hot wind, with plenty of firewood and grass. Here they made camp.

They had a fine supper, brought magically into being by Stephanie from the panniers of the pack outfit. Beans and bacon, canned corn, hot biscuits and coffee. While the girl cleared up afterward, Tam and Colly spread the sougans of the bedrolls, theirs on one side of the fire, the girl's on the other. They were sitting on the grassy bank, having a smoke, when the girl finished her chores. She sank gracefully to the grass, sighing.

In the silence Tam felt that this was a moment suspended between yesterday and tomorrow, the peace of it finely balanced, which would not likely last beyond the dawn. But now the air, cool, pleasantly scented by musty grass and pungent sage, was tinted with gold and flame from the dropping sunset, now fading into orange, and umber, and just before the vanishing of light, a glowing purple. But even at the end of light it was not fully dark.

Colly yawned, breaking the spell. "I'm for bed," he announced. "Tam, check the hosses before ye turn in. That Jimsey, I swear, kin untie knots."

Beside the dying fire, he wrestled off his boots, laid aside vest and jacket. Soon he was a bulky mound under his sougans, his head pillowed on his saddle.

Tam stood up, yawning, realizing how weary he was. "I'm hot and dirty and my hide is worn off in spots," he told Stephanie. "When I check the horses, I'm going to take a bath, if the pond is deep enough."

"It is," she said, finding him soap and a towel. She handed him a small jar. "Rub this on the sore spots, Tam; it will ease them. It's bear grease." She was smiling in the faint glow of the firelight, as he walked away.

Beyond the fire, the night seemed as dark as a mine pit. But as he neared the end of the pond where the horses were tethered in the long grass, he was beginning to see by the starlight and afterglow, enough, at least, to avoid obstacles. He found the five dark bulks that were the horses, checked each picket rope, finding them intact as the horses snorted.

By a tall, wedge-shaped tree that marked the end of the pond, Tam stripped, shivering a little in the coolness of the night air. Naked, he waded through the soft mud of the margin, finding with some surprise the pond rapidly deepening to his hips. He drew a deep breath and flung himself headlong into the cool water, gasping with the shock of it. Back in shallower water, he soaped himself thoroughly, rinsing away the grime and the sweat of the long day. He tossed the soap to the bank and launched out toward the center of the pool, finding it well beyond a man's depth as it dropped away toward the center. He swam for a minute or two, then splashed toward the white glow of the towel that marked his entry.

He dried off, and was working the bear grease into the chafed skin of his thighs when he heard a slight noise. He lifted his head. Skunk, no doubt, Tam thought. He grinned at the picture of him coming back into camp saturated with the essence of polecat. The night went quiet again.

Then one of the horses snorted. By some instinct, Tam turned, dropping to one knee. The movement saved his life. The arm that came for his throat hit his damp chin instead, slipping away. A rough body slammed against Tam, a man's body rank with the smell of sweat and booze and old tobacco. Tam fell away, reaching out to catch and hold a corded wrist.

"Leggo me!" the man grunted. He jerked his weight, trying to pull free. "Bryce! Over here! I've got the son of a bitch!"

Panic rising in him, Tam surged back, feeling the soft bank of the pond under his bare feet. The hard boot of his assailant ground cruelly into his foot. Tam groaned, and threw himself backward, dragging the man with him. There was a muffled yell as they splashed into the chill water. Tam, slipping in the ooze of the bottom, found footing. He saw the gleam of steel in the starlight, and caught the man's wrist in both hands.

"Bryce! Get over here and help me with this wildcat!" the man called out, trying to jerk free.

"Where in hell are you?" another voice called.

Can't handle two, for certain, Tam thought in desperation. With the strength of terror, he drove under the man's upraised arm, twisted, and pulled, in a mighty hip throw. The man sailed over him, striking the deep water with a tremendous splash. Tam launched out in his overhand stroke for the safety of the far bank. But a threshing hand caught him, held him like a steel clamp. Tam dived, pulling the man under the surface with him. When the grip relaxed, he pulled free.

The man came up coughing. "Cain't—cain't swim!" he gasped.

"Then drop the knife," Tam said.

Instead the man lunged. Tam, seized by a fury such as he had never known, rode the man down, driving him into the slime of the bottom, holding him there while the air bubbled past him, the man's lungs filling. In his own element, Tam stayed down until the struggle lessened, the man was still. With the last of his breath, Tam kicked to the surface, gasping for air.

"Lisbon?" asked a voice from the bank. Tam did not answer.

Flame gouted, and lead slashed the water close to Tam. He dived, swimming underwater toward the upper end of the pond. He trod water, looking toward their camp, listening. There was no sound, and panic shook him. Had the men already overrun the camp? What of Colly? What of Stephanie? The fury flared again. Against all caution, against all principle, Tam cut toward the marker tree. Unarmed and naked, he still was moving to the attack. He was tiring now, the cold striking a peculiar lassitude into his muscles. He swam on. With my bare hands, he thought . . .

"Tam, you all right?"

Tam's heart leaped, for it was Colly's voice. He kicked high and called out, "Look out! There's another one!"

A gun flared in the darkness like a red flower. From Devoe's position a rifle crashed twice. Beyond the marker tree at the end of the pond rose an insane, bubbling yell. It dropped into silence.

"I got the varmint, Tam!" Colly yelled. "No sign of any more. You can come ashore. Over here!"

Tam went into a fast stroke, churning toward the marker tree. His knees struck the soft mud and he stood up. His body felt heavy and weak without the support of the water. He lurched up the bank, feeling grass beneath his bare feet.

There was the scratch of a match. In a moment a ship's lantern was spreading its yellow glow as Devoe held it high.

"By the Lord, Tam, I didn't look to see you alive," he said.

"Glad—to be," Tam said thickly. "Drowned—one of 'em."

There was the sound of surf in his ears. He moved closer to the light, but it grew dimmer. Now he saw Stephanie, standing beside her father, concern in her great dark eyes. She shouldn't be here. Tam thought. My—clothes—Then his knees folded under him. His last sensation was the pleasant scratchy softness of the grass against his cheek. Then darkness.

# 10

Tam's mind wandered groping through a maze of unrelated facts, touching one lightly, then another. It did not try hard, the answers just beyond its grasp. Now the floating softness coalesced; with the magic of a kaleidoscope the pattern fell into place. He remembered the fight in the dark, the cold waters of the pond, the futile face of the drowned man. Then the circle of lantern light, Colly's grave face. And beyond the light, Stephanie. At that memory he squirmed a little, and opened his eyes.

He found the sky gray with dawn. Raising up in his cocoon of blankets, he felt pain bite sharp along his ribs. A soft hand touched his forehead, gently forcing him back.

"Easy, Tam," came Stephanie's voice. "How do you feel?"

"My back hurts," he told her. "Steve, what happened?"

"Two men, Lisbon Frank and Bryce Flinn, trailed us here. They tried to kill you—they were Clee Strike's men. The Portuguese cut you with a knife. You lost a lot of blood."

"So that's why I fainted," he said.

In the half-light, the girl's face was harsh and beautiful. "That's why," she said. "Tam you fight wickedly. You drowned the Portuguese."

Tam knew he should have felt shock. Instead, he felt a surge of grim satisfaction. "He had it coming. What happened to the other?"

"He fired at Papa. Papa shot him dead. Though they were pagan devils, Papa is out now giving them Christian burial. It was not easy getting Lisbon Frank out of the pond." She smiled wanly. "Papa swore a blue streak when he had to wade out into that cold water."

Tam looked at her calm face, marveling at her acceptance of violence, of sudden death. He thought back to those moments of swirling action. Nothing like it had ever happened to him before. He felt pride rise in him—he had been taken by surprise, naked and unarmed, yet he had bested his attacker, killed him. There had been, he knew, a measure of luck in it. But he had played his hand as it had been dealt to him, and won. What more could any man do, even Cleland Strike?

I know now, he thought, how Colly felt about Dirty Nose lying dead in the street in Benton. This world will be a hell of a lot better without Lisbon Frank and Flinn. My doings, and on my head be it. He dozed a little.

Stephanie stirred and Tam awoke. He heard her say, "Did you take care of—of them?"

Colly said: "They're safe under the prairie. Not six feet under; that would be too much to ask a man in this gumbo soil. But I added a few rocks to weight 'em down, so the coyotes won't be gnawin' their bones for a while. How's Tam?"

Tam raised up on an elbow, this time finding the pain more bearable. Stephanie gave him a cup filled with brown liquid. He drained it. In a minute or two the pain eased.

Colly hunkered down beside the bed. "Feelin' better, son? Stephanie's by way of bein' a medicine woman. She'll have you on your feet in no time." He fumbled in a vest pocket. "Found ye a souvenir, Tam. Kinda the spoils of victory. I found it on the Portugee before I planted him."

Tam took the finely made, vicious little pistol and examined it.

"What kind of gun is this?" he asked.

"Double derringer, forty-one caliber," Colly told him. "Favorite with gamblers, a real hideout gun. Keep it, Tam. It might save your life sometime."

"I don't know if I would have the fortitude to shoot a man," Tam said doubtfully.

"Ruther drown 'em, eh?" Colly said, with a chuckle.

The long day and the night drifted away. The following morning Stephanie examined Tam's wound and vetoed traveling for another day. She told her father: "In the heat of the summer it is so easy for blood poisoning to set in, I'd rather wait. One more day won't hurt anything."

"But tarnation, Stevie," Colly said glumly, "the Métis—no tellin' what them dam' fools is lettin' Clee Strike talk them into. We ought to be riding fer the border."

"Then you go ahead," Stephanie said impishly. "I'll stay here on the Marias with Tam until he can ride again."

"What!" Colly exploded. "Why, girl, you wouldn't have no more repitation than a Benton honkytonk gal. Are you loony?"

"Why, Papa, you know Tam is a perfect gentleman."

Colly grinned sourly at Tam. "Mebbe. But he's got more'n branch water in his veins. Which means it ain't safe to leave him alone very long with a pretty Métisse like you."

It was the girl's turn to become flustered. She stalked away from them, her back an uncompromising line.

Her father laughed. "Tam, better cure up quick. Because we ride north in the morning, in spite of hell, high water, or Stevie. There's death down the wind, boy, and fire along the border; I kin smell it."

Tam awoke the following morning refreshed and feeling himself again. He let Stephanie bandage his side, finding most of the soreness gone. The girl used strips of linen torn, he suspected, from some of her own garments. It embarrassed him a little, to have her working on his bared torso, but she had the competent, impersonal air of a doctor.

"Told ye she could cure anything," Colly said, pride in his voice.

Stephanie secured the end of the bandage and stepped back. "I studied all of it I could in school," she said. "I know I can be a real help to my people. Most of all I'd like to be a real doctor, but there is little hope of that. But I think I've made you as good as new, Tam, barring some decorations. Here's your shirt."

The bandage served Tam well during the long day. It was late when they angled up a coulee, with the Three Buttes looming huge to the north. Their trail was well marked, the hoofprints of horses shod and unshod, the ruts of wagon tracks, the wide parallel scrape marks of a travois or two. The coulee narrowed, pinching in on the trail.

With the suddenness of a conjuring trick, two men blocked the trail, their Winchesters ready. Colly Devoe called a greeting in the patois and rode toward them. The rifles eased off, and the men exchanged a rapid spate of words with Devoe. It was faster than Tam's present fluency in the Métis tongue could follow. Colly Devoe passed over a sack of Bull Durham.

"That does it," Stephanie said as the sentries began rolling brown-paper cigarettes.

"A modern pipe of peace," Tam said. "Once upon a time men broke bread or ate another's salt. Now they fire up a quirly."

"Another of the mysterious rites of grown men," Stephanie said.

Colly Devoe waved a negligent signal. "Joe Bonheur and Henri Fouclet," he said with a flick of the thumb toward the two sentries. "They're down from Batouche to join Pierre LaCroix."

The men smiled greeting. They bowed low to Stephanie.

"'Jour, mam'selle, m'sieu," they said.

With a wave of the hand they passed the sentries. Tam was happy that the end of the trip was near, for the pain of his wound was now a continual ache, biting into muscle and bone. It was bearable, but he would be glad to find a place to lie down and rest.

The size of the Métis camp surprised him. Along a creek bottom many tents and wickiups and lodges were strung out. Tam made a quick estimate, guessing that there must be five hundred people camped here. And, he thought, almost as many dogs. Dogs that barked and yelped and bayed around them, spooking the horses, just missing being stepped on time and time again. The pack escorted them to the center of the camp.

Tam saw that the large tent in the middle was the same Sibley that had dominated the old Métis camp along the Missouri. The flap was thrust open, and Gabriel Valier came out. He raised a hand in greeting. His face was grave.

"An honor, m'sieu's, Mam'selle Stephanie, that you visit our encampment," he said, with a courtly bow.

"More than a visit," Colly Devoe said. "We hear that there are big doin's afoot. We'd like to pitch our tent with the Bois Brûlés fer a spell."

Valier rubbed his beard. "The Burntwood People have few friends these days, but we count you among them. Most certainly you may camp with us." He made a slight gesture. From the shadows sprang a young boy, lithe as a puma, slat-ribbed, grinning at them. He stood there, his skin the golden glow of an Etruscan bronze, saying nothing.

"Antoine, they need a place with good wood and water," Valier directed. "Perhaps the far end of the little pond. M'sieu's, when you are settled, you come back and make talk, no?"

"Not tonight, Gabriel. We are weary, and M'sieu' Barrie has been wounded. In the morning, after breakfast. Is LaCroix in camp?"

Tam thought Valier looked troubled as he shook his head.

"He is at the—he is away. That is why we have no formal council tonight. As you know, Pierre is our governor."

"So he's at Strike's camp," Devoe said. "No matter, Gabriel. We know pretty much what goes on. But we must see him tomorrow."

"I think—I suppose he will be back tomorrow," Valier said. He frowned, plucking at his beard. "It is hard, m'sieu's, that in so many things Pierre keeps his own counsel. I am much in the dark. Which may be as well, for I find things disturbing."

"So do we," Colly said. "We'll see you in the morning, Gabriel, and talk over things. If you agree, we'll lay our knowledge before the council tomorrow night. It might change things."

"I fear not," Valier said. "But we must try." He motioned to the boy. "Lead the way, Antoine. You know the small deep pond. And, you scamp, do not let me catch you and your friends swimming there again naked, for mam'selle camps nearby."

The golden lad stood on one foot like an ibis, scratching his leg with a prehensile toe of the other foot. He spoke for the first time. "It would not be fitting," he said, and darted away, startled by his own temerity. They followed him.

The sun was high in the sky when Sophie Valier popped her whip over the ears of the team, the new team they had picked up at a ranch house at dawn. The buggy went storming down the hill with Sophie braced against the dashboard and Dove hanging on in desperation. A man rose out of the grass, a startled look on his face, but they were past him and among the tents before he could raise his rifle to his shoulder. They plunged down the street of tents, Sophie managing to stop the horses at the very end of it. The Métisse jumped down, with no visible signs that she had driven all night. She gave Dove a triumphant glance.

"We are here, woman," she said.

Dove climbed down slowly, her body one great ache. Under her clothing she was chafed and sweaty. Her hands were caked and gritty, her face, she knew, as dirty as a street gamin's. She moved stiffly, like an old woman. Holding to the buggy, she managed to straighten up. She looked at the tent, the largest of all on this street of tents. This would be her husband's, she knew. Summoning all her courage, she forced herself to walk straight and erect past the Métisse and into the tent.

The front, half-boarded, was partitioned off from the rear by a canvas wall. She walked across the wooden floor and pushed the canvas aside. The room was furnished, she saw vaguely. But there was only one thing she was interested in. She collapsed across the nearer of the two cots, buried her face in the pillow, and, in spite of heat, dirt, and discomfort, was asleep in five seconds.

# 11

Dove was young. When she had collapsed into bed, she had thought she would never get up again. But the next morning she had recovered and was taking an interest in her surroundings. This Hay Lake camp, as her husband had called it, was a nondescript affair. Some thirty tents, of various sizes and mainly the worse for wear, made up its street. A larger tent marked each end of the street, at one end the cookhouse and dining room, at the other the command tent and living quarters of Cleland Strike.

Dove ventured the length of the company street. She hurried back to her tent with her cheeks hot with anger and her skin crawling. Wait until I tell Clee, she raged. The way those unkempt rascals looked at me, the remarks they made loud enough for me to hear! She flung herself down on the cot, rubbing her flaming cheeks. She had never heard such brutal earthiness in her life before.

But gradually her anger ebbed away. Common sense intervened. She was beginning to learn something of the strange man who was her husband. And she was reasonably sure that he would savor her indignation, laughing at the joke of it. He might even, with that thin streak of cruelty that showed in him, make her repeat what the men had said. No, Strike needed these fighting men, and they were not the type to take kindly to discipline. They were mercenaries. Better if she kept her mouth closed.

She had walked the whole length of the street, after the first hundred feet wanting to turn and run, but persisting with the stiff-necked pride of the Demarests. She had gone into the mess tent, looked around and walked back, alone under the eyes of a good part of Strike's two hundred men. She shivered a little at the memory, feeling the impact of their bold stares.

She had no idea where her husband had recruited this motley army. They are, she thought, perfectly suited to his purpose. All of them wear that reckless air; they have a brutal shine in their eyes. She thought of an expression she had overhead on a street in Benton: "He's got that go-to-hell look about him." And Dove knew now what the speaker had meant. These men had seen better days and worse; they were lean and corded and tense, with the whipcord toughness of a pack of hunting hounds. Though in the look of some of them, Dove saw the signs of corrosion and decay, as if the spirit did not match the outward appearance.

Dove was thankful that Sophie Valier, stolid as she was, slept nearby, in a small tent behind the command tent. Dove roused herself now, and left the tent by the screen door at the rear. She let herself out silently, pausing to glance about her before she hurried down the path. From the center of the camp she could hear the bark of commands, as the officers tried to instill some sense of order into the movements of this mob of men.

Coming back a little later, she was unobserved. To save her precious shoes she was wearing a pair of moccasins Sophie Valier had made for her. She eased open the screen, stepped inside, and shut it without a sound, conscious of a hum of voices in the main part of the tent.

She debated leaving again. But where could she go? And all morning she had felt slightly unwell. She lay down on the cot, loosening her basque waist. Beads of sweat sprang out on her forehead. She lay quiet and miserable.

In the quiet of the tent she could hear the spoken words beyond the partition. In spite of herself she began to listen.

"You can't tell me, LaCroix," her husband was saying, irritation in his voice, "that every man-jack in your band doesn't already have a rifle. And a goodly stock of powder and ball for it, too."

"I do not deny that, M'sieu' Strike," LaCroix said calmly. "But what rifles! Many of them Hudson's Bay trade guns, many muzzle-loaders. A few are even flintlocks, or flintlocks converted for percussion caps. And there are a few huge Sharps, heavy as anvils. Fine guns, m'sieu', for shoot the buffalo from a stand. But to kill men—then better weapons we must have."

Strike grunted. The voice of Chance Flagg broke in. "LaCroix, assuming it were possible for us to get hold of such material, what would be the absolute minimum that would satisfy your men?"

Dove lifted her head. Chance Flagg was the nominal commanding officer of this crude little army. He was tall and lean and fined down like many of the others, but even more bitter than most, a cashiered West Pointer, Dove guessed. Flagg was handsome in his stony way, and in their short encounter earlier he had been most pleasant to her. More friendly, she had to admit, than her own husband, who was terse, preoccupied, wrapped in clouds of glory.

LaCroix was answering. "We have but forty repeating rifles. For them, each one a hundred cartridges of forty-four caliber. For my other men, a hundred and fifty new repeaters, with one hundred cartridges each. And two cannon—my men love the little cannon. They will not move without them. Those are my minimum terms, Major Flagg—a hundred and fifty new rifles, twenty thousand cartridges, two cannon. We will furnish our own horses, our own food—and our own knives."

"You ask the impossible!" Strike snapped. "Don't you realize, LaCroix, that this will cost a fortune? Thirty thousand dollars wouldn't cover it, delivered here."

"What does cost concern me?" There was acid in the words of LaCroix. "You promised—you have guaranteed—that when I found two hundred fighting Métis to spearhead your revolt, you would furnish the money and the arms, and an equal band of trained men. M'sieu' Strike, we hold you to that promise."

"If I knew you would…" Strike said, and stopped. Dove heard his chair scrape back, heard the thud of his boots as he paced the wood floor. "I keep my promises," he flung at LaCroix. "How do I know you will keep yours? You have promised me the fur concession, the mining concession, a monopoly on all means of transportation. But when you are in power, you can keep my men guarding the frontier, fighting off the Dominion forces, while you grow stronger. How do I know you will not renege?"

"You have the word of a Métis," LaCroix said, with dangerous quietness. "M'sieu', this enterprise is based on mutual trust. But it is easier to trust when you have equal forces. Most of your men are well armed. When my men are armed equally, why then we will trust each other!"

"Are you threatening me, LaCroix? Do you want to pull out of the plan? Then go ahead. I can get Valier. I can get Louis Riel."

LaCroix laughed. "I think not, m'sieu'. Of a surety the Bois Brûlés would follow my good Gabriel Valier. But Gabriel is a practical man. He is not sure in his heart that our crusade will succeed. Though it must, I tell you it must succeed …." His voice rose high, almost breaking, momentarily pitched like the voice of a fanatic. Then he grew calm. "Nor would Gabriel consent to paying tribute later, as I have agreed to pay. As for Riel … M'sieu', Louis Riel is a saint, a dreamer of dreams. He uses the law to get justice from Old Tomorrow, the man Macdonald. He will never give up the cause of the Métis. But he will go along the legal way until all resources are exhausted before he will take up arms again. This is too slow for me. M'sieu', I am a dreamer, I am also a practical man. I believe we will win. So, m'sieu', do not talk to me of Valier and Riel. Both of them may be better men than Pierre LaCroix, but they lack a certain hard ruthlessness of spirit that will, to win its ends, even make an alliance with such a *cochon* as you, M'sieu' Strike!"

"Why, you son of a bitch!" Strike rasped. Dove heard the sound of a scuffle. Chance Flagg cried out, "No, no, Clee!"

There was the noise of a chair falling over, and the heavy breathing of the men. Flagg said: "We can't stand any personal feud; there's too much at stake. Come to your senses. None of us can back out now, and you both know it. Sit down here."

"He is right, M'sieu' Strike," LaCroix said tensely.

"Damn it, he is," Strike said. "All right. I'll get rifles for you. And ammunition, and the two cannon. Some way. But, LaCroix—you march the day after you get them. By the following sunset I want every policeman of the Royal Mounted in Northwest Canada dead or behind bars."

"That is a bargain," LaCroix said. "Name the day."

"The 20th of August."

Chance Flagg whistled softly. "That's damned few days," he said.

I like this man Valier, Tam thought. Though he has a romantic turn of mind, he's as solid as a granite boulder. He is idealist enough to believe in the destiny of the Métis nation, but he can think straight enough to see the tremendous odds. He will, I think, do the best thing for his people. He would not be one to send men to death with no chance of winning justice for his people.

Since time was running out, Colly and Tam had gone to Valier with the statements of Clip O'Boyle. LaCroix was still away at the Hay Lake camp.

"I am not much surprised," Valier said gravely, when they were done. "Strike I do not trust. That is why my sister, Sophie, is housekeeper for the man. She picks up small bits of information now and again. Strike treats her well because she is good cook. But Sophie, she is afraid of his terrible temper."

"Like everyone that knows the man," Colly Devoe said. "He could be a great man, Gabriel, but there's something wrong in his nature. He's like a railroad engyne runnin' wild off its track, smashin' every pore divil in his road."

"I do not know what is an *engyne*," Valier said, puffing at his stubby pipe, "but I think he is like the bull moose, who charge everything in the forest. But again, this Strike is like the carcajou, wily and cunning, his mind a secret thing."

"He is no friend of mine," Tam said. "But he is a leader. Will he lead your people straight, Gabriel?

The Métis leader stared at him, unwinking. He puffed on his pipe, then took it from his lips. He pointed the stem at Tam. "M'sieu' Barrie, our kinsmen across the border will not give up easily what they have won by their hard work, their skill—aye, even their blood. None of the Métis fear Strike. If he give us the rifle, the ammunition, we follow him. We are a proud people; we cannot live for slave. Better die quick, brave, and strong, then be tie up like dumb oxen."

"If the Métis follow Clee Strike, plenty of them will die," Tam said bluntly. "Gabriel, do you realize the forces that will be arrayed against the Métis? No matter how brave and strong your people are…"

Valier grunted deep in his throat. "You think, young Barrie, you are saying things new to me? I know those things. And yet they are not the most deadly dangers to the success of rebellion."

"I don't understand," Tam said.

"The danger is in the nature of these my people. Forty years ago, or thirty, the Bois Brûlés were tireless on the trail, masters of the hunt. Even ten years ago, when they rose up in Manitoba, they were strong enough to win. But even then they were not strong like in the old times." He paused, staring out across the vacant land. He looked back, straight at Tam. "M'sieu', the Métis are no longer the grand *voyageurs*. Strong of body, yes. Good shots, good trackers, yes. But the spirit, it is not so strong as when life was a hard struggle. The Métis love too much the dance, the drink, the making of love and babies. They get angry, they fight, but like small boys they soon forget why. The man for a fight is bitter hungry—he hate hard and he fight hard. My people, they are fine and good, but their spirit has grown soft. Not one of them can sing Falcon's Song."

Colly Devoe said: "I remember that one—'Sing the glory of all the Bois Brûlés.' You think your lads won't fight, Gabriel?"

Frowning, Valier shook his head. "The Métis will fight fiercely and most brave. They will carry the battle with an air; but then, my friend, will they fall away, weary? If they do, all the fruits of victory will fall to Strike, as ripe apples fall from the tree. The last state of my people will be worse than the first."

"What should we do about it?" Colly Devoe asked.

"We must wait," Valier said. "As long as there is a chance of success, I must go with my people. If they go the wrong course, taking the road to certain disaster, I must do what I can to save them."

"You'll speak up in the council?" Tam asked.

"I will demand sureties from Strike. But whether Pierre—" he broke off. He shook his head. "We must wait until Pierre returns. But I feel deadly danger all around us." There was sadness in Valier's voice. He walked slowly away, head bowed, toward the main camp.

Late that afternoon, Pierre LaCroix rode into camp with a small band of Canadian Métis. Though he looked tired, there was an air of triumph about the man. A little later the word passed that there would be a council that night.

"I'm going," Stephanie said.

"No women at council, Stevie," her father said. "You know that."

"I will not speak out, Papa. But I must hear. I am afraid, afraid for the Burntwood People. Somehow they must learn what terrible forces will be arrayed against them. They will be crushed, and more—for every man of the police who is killed, the gallows will groan with the weight of the men of the Bois Brûlés. Killing is not the answer, Papa."

"Never has been," Colly Devoe said.

"All we can do is to see what happens at the council," Tam said. "But LaCroix has ambitions as well as Strike. I'm afraid of what might happen."

The Métis are a voluble people. That night, when the council met, they were made more voluble by excitement. The small band of Canadian Métis who had come in with LaCroix had brought new stories, new rumors of the impending start of the land survey, which would strip the Bois Brûlés of their Canadian lands. The young men were fired to anger. They made impassioned speeches, cheering each speaker until the night echoed.

Tam, watching LaCroix, saw a cold smile flit over the man's ascetic face from time to time. But only when the spate of oratory had worn itself thin did he move to the forefront. The firelight cast a red glow on his skin; it made his eyes shine with a strange glow, as well. He held up his hand for quiet.

"My people! The time has come. With our own strong hands we will end injustice. This is our hour of glory. In but a few short days we will launch a war of extermination upon our oppressors. We will destroy these hostile men!" The crowd roared. LaCroix held up his hand again. He resumed in a more controlled voice. "Seven years—seven long years we have been petitioning Ottawa for a commission to look into our complaints. There is still no commission. Instead, these our brothers, from the north, tell us that soon the government's surveyors are coming, surveying on the new plan which we despise, taking from our people the riverfront lots won with sacrifice and blood. So today, men of the Bois Brûlé, we stand out before the world as free men. We march soon to join our kinsmen in their struggle for justice. The trained fighting men of M'sieu' Strike will join us, bringing new rifles, plenty of ammunition. And—listen, my brothers—for us,

THE BURNTWOOD MEN

two cannon! Listen then for the word to come—'*Marchons! Au victoire!*'"

LaCroix stepped back, smiling. Men leaped to their feet, shouting wildly. They surged around LaCroix. Tam found himself moving forward. He had been able to follow most of the speech, though it tested his new found knowledge of the Métis tongue. It appalled him—he wanted to force his way to the front, to demand a hearing. To tell these simple people of the brigades and the legions that would come to overwhelm them in the end, to tell them of the death and the sorrow which awaited them at the end of this path to glory.

But Tam did nothing of the kind. He sat, unmoving, detesting his cowardice, though he knew in his heart that nothing he could say would have any effect on these excited men. But he knew, as well, that it was his duty, as a man, to try.

"When? When?" the shout went up.

LaCroix raised his hand. "August 21st!" he shouted.

A sudden hush came over the mob. It was one thing to plan a fiery march on the Northwest Territories; it was another to be faced with a day and hour. But the Métis were not men to be discouraged by a word. The shouting raised louder. Logs went onto the fire. Someone started an impromptu dance. The others joined in, whooping and singing.

Tam saw Gabriel Valier struggle through the press. He spoke to LaCroix, but whatever Valier said made the governor shake his head. Valier was arguing vehemently, but LaCroix, still with that enigmatic smile on his face, continued to shake his head. Finally Valier, his face stormy, came back through the crowd to join Tam and Colly Devoe.

They walked away from the crowd, toward the Devoe camp at the far pond. Stephanie came hurrying up to join them. They made their way along the path, no one speaking. At the bend of the trail, Valier stopped and looked back.

"See them—a bunch of boys let out of school. Ready for fight or frolic, maybe both. But not the ones to fight a war, these. To raid, to make the daring charge, yes. But for the long stupid waiting of war, for the hot days and the cold nights when nothing happens, no. Colly, I must find a way to stop these foolish ones before they cross the border, before they harm one man of the Mounted Police. LaCroix will not listen, he is satisfy'. He hate the Canadians."

They reached the little camp. Devoe tossed an armful of sticks on the embers of the campfire. As they blazed into light, Tam saw the serious face of Stephanie, the scowl on the face of Gabriel Valier. The Métis leader pulled at his beard.

A sudden thought came to Tam. "Would they march without the promised arms? Without the cannon?"

Valier's head came up. "Tam Barrie, many of those dancing yonder"—he jerked a thumb toward the distant camp—"would drop away like rabbits if they did not march with new repeating rifles. And since Fort Garry, they love the cannon. These are foolish lads, but they know the Mounted Police are well trained and well armed. They want to be equipped as well as their enemy."

"If the arms shipment could be intercepted..." Tam said.

Colly Devoe slapped his thigh. "Tam, you've got the ticket. The way it's timed, the shipment must be comin' from the south. If we could only run it off..."

Stephanie spoke then. "It will be guarded well, and its route will be secret. Strike knows that every man in the Whoop-Up hates the thought of arms shipments. The Army, the trading houses, the steamboat men, the freighters—all of them dread seeing modem weapons seeping into the hands of renegades."

"How could we find out? Gabriel, think that sister of yours might pass us the word?"

"If she knew it, Colly," Valier said. "It would not be easy for her to get away from Hay Lake. Especially since this girl who calls herself Mrs. Strike is ailing, or so LaCroix says."

"Dove is ill?" Tam asked. The feeling he had put aside surged back in him. Dove, the wayward, imperious one, could look out for herself on her home grounds. But out here on the great prairie, alone and sick—Tam had looked out for Dove before. He must do it again. "I've got to go to her," he said.

Stephanie looked at him oddly. Her head was high. "You would be walking into certain death," she said. "Remember Lisbon Frank and Bryce Flinn."

"I'll take the chance," Tam said.

"Tam, you're tetched in the head ..." Colly began.

"Wait!" Stephanie cried. "There is one way, and it would give us a chance to talk to Sophie Valier. I am an herb woman, M'sieu' Valier. I will go to the Hay Lake camp to doctor the ailing wife of Strike. Tam can go with me as my brother, a medicine man of the Métis."

"'T'won't be what I'd call a safe proposition, Tam," Colly Devoe said, grinning. "But damn' if I don't think ye could make it. Your dark hair, skin burned by the sun, shave off that leetle cookie duster of yours and dress ye in Métis clothes, I b'lieve they'd pass ye fer a Métis if ye keep your mouth shut."

Tam felt himself hesitating. The tempting thought came— Dove has made her bed. Let her lie in it. I owe these half-savage people nothing. Why should I put my head into the lion's mouth for a mere matter of principle?

Then he knew it would not do. There were more than forms of ritual in the making of a man. At home, form and ritual might serve. Out here, in the Whoop-Up, the measure of a man cannot be skimped. And with a strange insight, it came to Tam that he was merging his own objectives with those of the Métis, that their wrongs had suddenly become very real and grave to him. Now this gay, brave people was embarking on a course of deadly danger. He felt that he must do whatever he could to prevent disaster from reaching them.

"I'll go," he said simply.

"Good! But play it cautious, you two. Don't go askin' too many questions; work with Sophie. She'll likely have the answers for you," Colly said.

"May *le Bon Dieu* go with you," Gabriel Valier said. "We must stop this supply of arms. For LaCroix said the first object of Strike was to kill all of the Mounted Police. LaCroix is not afraid; he says we will have the upper hand before we can suffer reprisals. But I am afraid—me, Gabriel Valier—for the Queen will never forgive such a deed. And the arm of the queen is long, m'sieu's. There will be no limit to the forces she will send in to revenge her men in scarlet tunics, if Strike has them murdered."

"Right you are, Gabriel," Colly said. "Wisht some of your people felt the same way."

"A few good, serious men do think that way," Valier said. "Enough to ride with us against the arms shipment, when we have learned by what way it comes. And I think many of the Métis, deep in their hearts, are not anxious to do murder, whether it is called revolt or insurrection or rebellion."

Colly put a hand on the shoulder of Tam and Stephanie. "As Gabriel said, God go with you. And keep out of the hands of that devil Strike. He would pay anything to get hold of either of you."

# 12

OVE HAD not seen or talked to Pierre LaCroix. Her husband
had explained to the Métis governor that Dove was ailing,
which was true enough, but it also served Strike as an excuse
to keep Dove from blurting out anything about his plans. Clee,
she thought, trusts no one. That is understandable, with the
appalling things he plans to carry out. To wipe out the Mounted
Police—that is more an act of murder than of war. She felt again
the creeping edge of terror at her new knowledge of the man she
thought she had known. Feeling alone and friendless, she felt the
tears of self-pity burning her eyelids.

She was too ill to eat supper, nor did the scowls of her husband make her feel any better. She undressed and went to bed
before the long twilight had gone. Though the narrow canvas cot
was uncomfortable, Dove fell into a fitful doze, finally dropping
off into sleep.

She wakened to a sliver of light around the canvas partition.
She heard a low hum of voices, and raised up on an elbow.

"...the whole country will be up," she heard Clee Strike say.
"We'll stick to the back roads, and turn north on the old smug-
gling trail across the Marias. Oh, I forget you did your soldiering
in the southwest, Flagg. That was a busy trail a few years ago. It's
still there, not as good as the Whoop-Up, but passable. It'll be
safe enough. We'll come through night after next."

Chance Flagg's deep voice asked a question. Dove, unable to
make out the words, stealthily put one bare foot, then the other,
to the cool boards. Shivering in her thin nightgown, she tiptoed

over to the partition. She bent her head close to the canvas, crouching low.

"You're the only other man who knows this, Flagg," Clee Strike was saying. "I've told the Métis, and this gang of range rats I'm paying good money to, that the arms are ready in a cache not far away. God knows what they'd do if they knew they were on a stinking little freight boat between Carroll and Benton."

"Why've you waited so long to deliver them?" Flagg asked.

"Hell, Chance, men who run guns have just one rule—cash on the barrel head. And with that fool of a Barrie around, I didn't dare draw bank funds for payment. Since I got rid of him, I have been able to draw out cash for the guns."

"They must be costing you a pretty penny."

"My dear major, guns on this frontier are almost literally worth their weight in gold. But with an empire at stake, who will stop to count the cost? This opportunity will never come again. I *will not miss it.* Mark my word, Flagg, they'll remember the name of Cleland Strike in the Northwest, in the world, for a long time."

Strike's voice had an intensity that was fanatical. Dove, shocked and faint at the knowledge of Tam Barrie's death, choked back a sob, and shivered at the sound of it.

"I believe you," Chance Flagg said. Was there a touch of irony in his tone? "How many men will we take to guard it?"

"Not you, Flagg. Since you are the only person I trust, you will stay here. I'll ride south at dawn with twenty men, men I have chosen myself. God help you, Flagg, if you betray my trust."

"I have few virtues," Flagg said drily. "One of them is that though I can be bought, I stay bought. I suppose your wife stays here?"

There was a trenchant pause. Strike asked flatly, "What is that to you?"

"Nothing. Except, mister, this is a damned wild and ugly place for a young girl, one raised in luxury. You ought to send her back to Benton, to safety."

Strike said in a cool voice: "Flagg, I bought you because you are the kind of villainous and unprincipled rascal that I needed for my desperate enterprise. But I do not now, nor will I in the future, require your interference in my personal affairs. My wife, Dove, is a pretty little featherhead, and I'm breaking her to my ways. But I'm still not sure she knows how to keep her mouth closed. And, Flagg, she is virtuous—she'd damned well better be. So don't go trying any gambits along those lines!"

"Strike, you insult your wife. She's a damned charming woman, and I like her. She's a deal smarter than you think. So let me give you just one piece of unwanted advice—don't ever let her hear about a pretty little Cree girl named Maria Easy Walker."

Strike ripped out an oath. "Where the hell did you get that? Are you trying to blackmail me?"

"Don't be asinine, Strike. Half the country knows you married that Indian girl at the point of a rifle and that it was legal and has never been dissolved. Just keep it from your wife. She must not be hurt by it."

Dove turned Flagg's words over in her mind, trying to comprehend them. He had said ... Then the import of it struck her with the harshness of a blow. The shock was almost physical. She staggered back to the cot, dizzy and sick. So this was the man she loved, this was the gay cavalier of the prairie, this was the prize she had worked so hard to snatch from under the noses of her rivals in Philadelphia! This man, all the while, had been married to an Indian girl.

Lying there, feeling recurrent waves of illness, Dove had to meet the facts head-on. She tested her own bitter logic, and knew it must be true. Cleland Strike would ever do what he wanted, take what he wanted, if it furthered his own ambition. He was like a machine driving toward a distant goal, a merciless juggernaut. She had been in his path and been crushed. She lay still, face buried in the pillow, crying silently.

She did not know how long the two men talked. She did hear them when they left the tent, with the lantern still burning. A desperate resolve shook Dove. She arose from the cot and went to her small trunk. Dizzily she searched out her riding habit, and, with little regard to appearance, managed to struggle into it. She wrapped a wool mantle around her shoulders and forced her feet into riding boots. Moving as quietly as she could, she went to the rear door of the tent.

Her hand was on the knob when the door was thrust open, forcing her back. Her hand went to her mouth. Cleland Strike came in. He stood staring at her in the faint light of the lantern.

"And where might you be going?" he asked harshly.

"I—I need some fresh air," she improvised. "I was going for a little walk."

"At this hour of night, in that outfit?" His hand reached out and seized her shoulder. "The truth—where have you been?"

"Most of the time, in Sophie's tent, down by the lake," she lied.

His hand tightened cruelly, and she cringed away.

"I just talked to Sophie. She's been back and forth to the cook tent, and hadn't seen you. Dove, you little devil, were you listening while I talked with Flagg?"

Suddenly fear dropped away from her. Smoldering rage took its place. She straightened.

"Yes. I heard every word," she defied him. "Cleland Strike, I admired you, I loved you. But I loved a man who never was, the shell of a man, handsome, gay, a shell that covered a mass of corruption. You are cruel and utterly selfish. You are a liar. It was a terrible shock to learn that a poor Indian girl is your lawful wife, not I. But now I'm glad."

Almost negligently, Strike thrust her away from him. The force of it threw her across the cot. She sat up. He came over to her, towering.

"There's some truth in what you heard, Dove," he said. "But that stupid young squaw meant nothing to me. Nor would anything have come of it if her father hadn't been listening to the priests. Give me time, Dove. Things are at too tight a pass at the moment to do anything, but later, I promise, I'll take care of it."

"By your usual method, Clee?" she asked silkily. "By assigning men with guns to search her out and kill her, as you did my cousin Tam Barrie?"

His hand flashed out, catching her alongside the head. The blow spun her from the cot onto the splintery floor. She lay there, her head ringing. She made no movement to get up. Strike reached down and hauled her to her feet. He knotted a hand into the front of her riding habit and jerked her against him. Fabric ripped, and Dove cried out.

"Keep quiet!" he ordered. "Now listen to me, you little fool! For the last time, I tell you I'll have no one stand in my way. Are you going to come to your senses?"

She tried to pull away. Her blouse ripped away under his hand, the straps of her camisole going with it. She cowered, trying to cover the nakedness of her bosom. Strike laughed at her, and caught her wrists, pinioning them, with one great hand. With the other he reached out and ripped the ruins of her clothing half off her body.

Dove Demarest had never in her young life received treatment like this. She reacted with utter fury.

"I'll break you, Clee Strike! I'll smash this terrible scheme of yours. I'll get word to the Mounted Police of the murders you intend. I'll get word to the Army; I'll tell them you're running guns and ammunition—"

He hit her, this time with closed fist. She staggered, moaning. With all the force she could muster, she caught him on the shin with the sole of her boot. He yelped at the pain of it. He came toward her, the ferocity in his face making her shrink with terror. She tried to run.

He caught her, seizing her pitiful rags. He began slapping her, coldly, methodically, rocking her head from one side to the other. Dove drifted in a red haze. The blows grew harder. She sagged. A heavy blow sent red stars flashing through her brain to burn back of her eyes. He must have closed his fist, she thought. Then the floor came up at her, and even in the torture of her body she could feel the single exquisite stab of a splinter, stabbing the palm of her hand. She lay there, the world a dull and distant murmur. She felt the vibration of Strike's step. She clasped her arms around her head.

She heard him grunt. Numbing pain drove into her side, once, twice. Then, mercifully, consciousness winked out.

Tam was riding a paint pony, no more than half broken. He was riding behind Stephanie's rangy bay along a prairie track that twisted toward the horizon. He felt strange, as if he were actually the Métis plainsman he had been dressed to resemble. He rubbed a knuckle over the smoothness of his upper lip, missing the mustache he had worn for many years.

As if reading his thoughts, Stephanie reined in her horse. "Tam, let me look at you by daylight," she said. She looked him over from the crown of his flat Stetson to the Cree moccasins on his feet. She was serious about it. Only when she was satisfied did she smile at him. "You'll do, if you don't talk a lot," she said. "Your hair is properly dark and long, your skin dyed. The shirt and trousers and leggings are true Métis. In fact, Tam, with the Assomption sash around your middle, you make quite a gallant figure. I'm sure you'll make the hearts of the Métisse girls flutter, when we get back to camp."

"You're teasing, Stevie," he said, but secretly he was pleased. "But you are the real thing—you've made yourself resemble all the lovely women of the Bois Brûlés. Though somehow you look older, heavier, more stolid. You've added twenty years."

"Perhaps the way I myself will look twenty years from now," she said, smiling. "A matter of acting, Tam. Both of us must act for our lives; we must *be* the people we pretend to be. Remember," she added with the old bitterness in her voice, "Clee Strike once knew me well enough to try to marry me. He's smart and he's dangerous. If we fall into his hands..." She stopped, shivering a little.

Tam leaned forward, his hands resting on the pommel of the saddle. "Stevie, I didn't sleep much, thinking of that very thing. I'm scared sick of him. Do you want to turn back?"

"You afraid, Tam? You who fought naked against Lisbon Frank in the pond by the Marias, and killed him? I don't believe it."

"It's true," he insisted. "Strike is too big for me. If I weren't afraid of having your father think me a coward, if it weren't for my cousin Dove..."

"You love this girl very much, Tam." Stephanie's voice was low.

"Why, I suppose I do..." Tam said, surprised.

"Come, we can't be sitting here; we must ride," Stephanie said. She urged her horse along the trail.

They came out on a ridge above the camp of the filibusters. Tam was surprised at the extent of it. From the number of tents, there could be two hundred men here. No wonder Strike thought he could break the back of the Mounted Police. With two hundred fighting men here, and the same number of fierce Métis, it would be possible to overrun all the forces north of the border, tough, well-trained policemen though they were.

Stephanie led the way down the slope, her horse trotting. If there were sentries around the perimeter of the camp, they did not challenge. He followed the girl down the street of tents, toward the large tent at the end, where an armed man was walking a guard post. He stopped them, rifle ready.

"Dees is w'ere the seeck woman is?" Stephanie asked, her accent thick.

The bold eyes of the sentry slid past the girl's moccasins, up her long tanned legs—for she was riding astride as the squaws rode, her skirt hiked up past her knees—and then tried to strip the buckskin from her body. Insolently he said: "Now, peachy, I don't know as I want to say. Come down off'n that horse and we'll step inter my tent and discuss it further."

Stephanie's stolid face did not change. "Our governeur, Pierre LaCroix, say there is w'ite woman seeck here. I herb woman; I come for cure woman." She untied a parfléche bag from the cantle of her saddle. Leaning forward, she shook it in the face of the sentry. "W'ite man, you want this woman should die?"

Anger was rising hot in Tam, but he kept himself within rigid control. He watched the sentry.

"Why, it makes no never-mind to me, one way or t'other," the man said. "She's Clee Strike's propitty. He give us orders to keep everybody but Sophie Valier outen that tent. So you …"

"What's the trouble here?" came a crisp voice.

Tam turned slowly, keeping his face impassive. The speaker was a tall lean man, the air of command written in his hawk face and his straight, disciplined body.

"These 'breeds tryin' to bust into the tent, Major," the sentry said.

Stephanie broke into a torrent of excited Métis. Wincing, the major held up his hand. Stephanie slowed down.

"… and since I am herb woman, Pierre LaCroix sent me, send my brudder wit' me to cure this woman."

The major looked at her doubtfully. He swung to give Tam a stern glance. Tam kept his face as unmoving as flint, his eyes remote and disinterested.

The major's eyes flicked toward the big tent. For a moment Tam saw raw suffering in the man's face.

"All right, Tex," the major said. "Mrs. Strike is a very sick girl, and she needs more than my rough knowledge of field medicine. Let them in. But no one else."

Stephanie acknowledged her thanks with a curt nod. Tam dismounted and took the reins of the horses. The girl sprang down and hurried into the tent, the parfléche bag held tight under her arm. Tam tied the horses and followed her.

The front of the tent, he saw, was cluttered with the usual stacks of papers. Even a guerrilla army, he thought, generates its piles of paper work. Hearing voices beyond the canvas partition, he thrust the flap aside.

Stephanie was at one side of a cot, leaning over. On the other was Sophie Valier, wringing out a cloth in a basin of stained water. The woman moaning on the cot, he saw, was Dove.

Anger surged up in Tam so fiercely he almost cried out. The man who had done this thing to Dove was not a man; he was a raging beast. For he had come within an ace of beating Dove Demarest to death.

# 13

DOVE'S FACE was one ghastly bruise, blue and purple and yellow-green. Her eyes were swollen almost closed. The slash of a raking ring seared one cheek. She moaned softly, her head turning from side to side. Tam knelt by the side of the bed.

Her hand clamped down tight on his with the strength of agony. Sweat glazed her forehead, and a pulse in her throat was racing. In a wordless plea, he looked up at Stephanie. She nodded.

She poured water into a tin cup and into it sifted, with extreme care, a small pinch of dried leaves from the parfléche bag. Tam slipped a hand behind Dove, raising her. Stephanie put the cup to Dove's lips. Gasping, the girl managed to drink, though some of the potion dribbled over her chin and down on to her bruised throat.

Slowly her breathing eased. Tam felt her pulse slowing. Her eyes came open, as if the lids bore an infinite weight. She looked around her with a puzzled stare, looked at Tam. The faintest of smiles came to her swollen lips.

"Tam," she whispered. "Tammie, and when I need you so."

He felt the quick tears come to his eyes. He smiled and placed a finger to his lips. He saw that she understood. Then Dove saw Sophie Valier. Terror twisted her bruised face.

"Get her away!" she said hoarsely. "She's Clee's woman."

Stephanie went to her knees beside Tam. "No, Mrs. Strike. She's your friend. She is working on our side."

Dove's head rolled to the side again. "No, no! She wants to kill the policemen."

Tam looked at the Métisse woman. There was nothing stolid now about Sophie Valier. Her face was marked by her pity for the girl. He smiled, making a little motion with his head. She nodded and moved to the back of the tent.

"Don't let this woman call me that, Tam," Dove pleaded.

"Call you what, my dear?"

"Not Mrs. Strike, Tam," Dove sobbed. "Clee—he was already married. He told me so. I thought—I thought I could handle him, Tam, handle any man, just as you used to jump to my orders. You're not like him, Tam. I didn't know there were men like Clee in the world."

He soothed her, patting her hand. Stephanie went to the rear of the tent and talked to Sophie Valier in low tones. She came back to the cot.

"Tam, this girl needs long and careful treatment. Besides the bruises you see, she has several broken ribs, and—and other injuries. I want to have you talk the major into letting us take her to the Métis camp."

"And Strike?" he asked.

"Strike is away. The girl is now deathly afraid of him, afraid he'll kill her." Then she added, bitterness in her voice, "From what I know of the man, I don't doubt he'll do it."

"The arms shipment?" he asked, looking at Sophie Valier.

"I don't know," the woman said. She motioned toward the girl on the bed, quiet now. "But she know. She say something..."

"The more reason to get her away." Stephanie said. "Go, Tam."

Tam stood up, dreading the walk into the bright sunlight. He thought of the weakness of his disguise. But it was a thing that had to be done. Perhaps those amateur theatricals back in Philadelphia so long ago would pay off at last. He squared his shoulders and pushed aside the flap of the tent.

A battered fatigue cap was the sentry's only concession to military dignity, but his rifle was businesslike. Tam brushed past him arrogantly and strode up to the major, where he was talking to some men beside another tent.

"You de governeur dis camp?" he demanded.

"I'm Major Flagg, yes. And I am in charge at present."

"Your woman mighty seeck, my sister say. She stay here, mebbeso die. My sister mus' take to Métis camp, make well."

Flagg shook his head. "That can't be. The woman is the wife of the—the commanding officer. You savvy?"

Tam shook his head. "She stay here, she die. My sister herb woman, she say so. Sick woman, she don' want to stay here; say she no wife of boss man. He married 'nuther woman, she say. Mus' take to Métis camp."

"Can't say as I blame her for being afraid," Flagg said. He gave Tam a calculating look. "What he did to that lovely girl—If I were only …" He stopped, looking off toward the south, his face rock-hard with anger. He beat his fist against his open palm.

"All right, take her. On my head be it. I haven't got a rig of any kind, but that's your problem. Move quickly. I hope by the time Strike gets back …" He caught himself. "Get her away within the hour. I won't be responsible after that."

Tam concealed his relief. He nodded in the impassive Métis way, and stalked back to the tent.

"But how will we take her, Tam? She can't ride. Somewhere there must be a buggy or a wagon …."

"We make travois," Sophie Valier said. "Plenty horses here. If we go slow, easy, we don' make the girl hurt."

"We'll try it, then," Stephanie said with some doubt.

"How bad is she, Stevie?" Tam asked.

"It's serious, for the next few days at least," Stephanie said. "After that—well, she's young and strong. If it were only the beating, I wouldn't worry. But her mind received a terrible shock. Beyond the truth she learned so suddenly, she was carrying Clee Strike's child."

"That man must be killed, Stephanie," Tam said coldly.

"He should. Tam, that child will not be born, now," Stephanie said, with the sadness of all women in the face of birth and death. "That beating he gave her ..."

The anger in Tam shook him until it nauseated him. He was trembling as he said to Sophie: "Come. Show me how to make the travois. I've got to get her out of here."

They came back to the tent with the travois in half an hour. It was a simple thing, the upper ends of two long poles fastening into sockets at each side of the horse's saddle, the lower ends lashed to crosspieces in a wide V, with a carrying pouch of canvas lashed between the crosspieces. The bottom ends of the poles dragged along the ground, the natural spring of the poles cushioning to some extent the roughness of the terrain. It would not be comfortable for Dove, but it would have to serve.

Tam wrapped the girl in blankets and carried her out of the tent. He placed her gently on the travois. Stephanie and Sophie secured her upon it with wide bands of cloth. The big gentle horse Tam had selected from the remuda stood patiently, unconcerned with the strange contraption at his heels.

The three mounted their horses, Tam taking the hackamore of the travois horse. Just then Major Flagg came around the corner of the tent. He stood looking down at the girl. Her eyes came open.

"Mrs. Strike—Dove—I can't tell you how sorry I am," he said. "But you are in good hands. If I live—if this business works out, perhaps I—we could be friends. Don't hate me, Dove."

"You have been my one friend, Chance," Dove whispered. "Look out for Clee. If he learns you let me leave, he will ... Chance, get out of this nightmare. Come with us. Now."

He shook his head. "Too late, Dove. I gave my word as a soldier. When the accounting comes ..." He stopped, looking at her with his heart in his eyes. He swung to Tam. "All right, all right, move on. Go, before I change my mind."

They moved out under the eyes of all the men in camp. Most of them were merely curious, a few pitying. Many of them were more interested in the bare legs of the two women as they rode astride their mounts. Tam never glanced aside. He led the horse up the hill, away from Hay Lake.

They went over the ridge. The camp dropped from sight. The grinding scape of the travois poles set Tam's nerves on edge. Now and again Dove would moan slightly as the movement of the litter plucked at some raw nerve. Tam breathed deep of the clean, dry air, feeling the first blazing anger at Strike's brutality settle into a solid wrath, a determined, objective hatred that he felt could never be appeased. It came to Tam as something of a surprise that he felt no fear at the thought of a clash with Cleland Strike. Had he, in the past few weeks, acquired a new sort of courage, or had one been forced upon him? It might fade when put to the test, he thought, but it's there. Perhaps it's because I've been shot at, stabbed, damn' near drowned, chased half across a county—not much more could happen to me. Man gets to be a fatalist after a while; he knows there's no way around things.

He glanced at Dove, silent now on the jolting travois. A wave of love and sympathy came over him—this girl, so young, so innocent; and a man utterly evil had beaten her almost to death, destroying the life he himself had planted in her body. This same man betraying the little Cree girl, who had no recourse except the ready rifle of her father. And the scars this man had put on the soul of Stephanie, who rode ahead now, her body straight, her face proud. The women he had betrayed, the men he had injured or killed—Tam clenched his fist on the reins. The man had tempted Fate.

Suddenly it came to Tam—the one thing that would break Cleland Strike, the thing that would be worse than death for him. If destruction came to this wild gamble of his, if it failed in a mighty collapse of cardboard and sand, Strike would be pulled down with it. His whole life was sunk into it. He had thrown his own life and fortunes, the assets of Seaboard & Continental, the lives and fortunes of a gentle people into his scheme. Frustrate it, and Cleland Strike would go down into the dust with it.

Tam was not particularly superstitious. But so many times his path had crossed with Strike's, so many times their interests had clashed, to meet and swing apart and come together again, that Tam felt there was something of fate in it. Before now, Tam had been evading it, trying to pull free. Instead, he had become more deeply tangled in the very sinews of the fortunes of Cleland Strike. Now he thought he knew why. From now on, he would work actively, with every tool he could command, to break Clee Strike. He would fight him to the last ditch, and if it killed Tam, if he was destined to lie in some unmarked grave on the timeless swell of the prairie, he would, at the least, have played a man's part.

With that decision, a strange peace came to Tam Barrie. There was no more need now for tortured thinking, for fear, for twisted terrors in the middle of the night. He rode now almost gaily, the black doubt lifted from his shoulders.

From time to time they stopped to take care of the injured girl, who dozed most of the time under the medication of herbs Stephanie was giving her. It was long after noon when they rode into the Métis camp. Children crowded around them curiously until Stephanie dispersed them with a gentle word. They made their way through the main camp to the Devoe tent beside the pond.

Tam lifted Dove in his arms and carried her into the tent. Half awake, she clung to him, moaning a little. He laid her on Stephanie's pallet. Stephanie put an arm under the girl's shoulders and gave her a cup of medicine. The girl came awake.

"Thank you, oh, thank you," Dove said. With an effort, she got control of herself. "Stephanie, hold me for a minute, please. In case I—I must tell Tam something."

"It will wait," Tam said, hoping she would rest.

"Tam, you idiot, I know what is important," she said with a touch of her old spirit. "I can sleep for a week after I have told you this, but not before. It will harm Clee Strike. It was so important that when Clee learned I had overheard it he did this to me, damn him! So I *must* tell you."

Tam went to one knee, the better to hear her.

"It's tomorrow night, Tam. With a guard of twenty men, Clee is bringing up a shipment of arms from somewhere along the river. They are arms for a raid in force across the Canadian border. Arms his ragtag army must have, arms the Métis must have. He is coming by the old smuggler trail, ten miles east of the Whoop-Up. Stop them, Tam. Stop him!"

Excitement rose in him. "How many wagons, Dove?"

She shook her head, and winced. "I don't know. Major Flagg would know. But he wouldn't tell. A good man, that man Flagg. I like him. Tam, Tam, you may be killed; Flagg may be killed. Such good men to lie dead upon the prairie, because of Cleland Strike. Stop him, Tam, somehow."

Tam stood up, "I'll try, Dove. Get some sleep now, like a good girl. We want you to get well." He gripped her hand for a moment.

Outside, Stephanie said to him: "I think she'll be all right. If the fever does not come, if she will rest her body and her mind."

Impulsively he said: "Stephanie, you're wonderful. I don't know words to thank you. This girl, alone and friendless in an unfriendly land, and you take her in and care for her."

"Should I have passed by on the other side?" she asked gravely. And added, almost inaudibly, "Besides, you asked me, Tam."

His eyes met hers. She gave him back a direct look; there was no coyness in it. The warm color rose in her tanned cheeks. Slowly he released her hand. He turned away. What is in her mind? he wondered. But it doesn't matter, as long as Dove will be all right.

He found Colly Devoe and Gabriel Valier by the pond, in the shade of a tree. He hunkered down beside them.

"The girl all right?" Colly asked.

"She's had the grandfather of all beatings," Tam said, "but Stevie thinks she'll make it. She's bruised from head to toe, a couple of ribs broken, and she lost the child she was carrying—Strike's child. Wasn't for Stephanie, though, I doubt if she'd made it through the day. She's resting now."

"Strike, eh? Tam, he's a fiend in human form, that man. Everything he touches comes to trouble. You learn anything?"

"Some," Tam said, with an air of nonchalance. "Strike hasn't got the arms and ammunition. He's coming up with them tomorrow night."

Devoe gaped. Gabriel Valier sat up, his stubby pipe falling unheeded to the grass.

"By what road?" he asked.

"The old smuggler trail, east of the Whoop-Up."

"That trail I know," Valier said tersely. "M'sieu's, this is our chance to stop Strike."

"How many men will Strike have? Did the gal say?" Devoe asked.

"Twenty in the escort, she thinks. With Strike and the teamsters, probably twenty-five in all. Picked fighting men, Colly."

"That tears it," Devoe said. "Ain't over six, eight men we could trust in all the camp, besides the three of us. Rest of 'em would go runnin' to LaCroix and spill the beans."

"After all, he *is* governor, Colly," Valier said, relighting his pipe. "They do not see that they are putting their heads in the Queen's noose, if they harm her men of the Police."

"They better wake up, then," Colly grunted. "How many can we muster for this job, Gabriel? Name them."

"The two Laurier boys. And Ouellette and Pinsonneault: they are relat' to the Easy Walkers; they hate Strike. Maybe one, two more."

"It might work," Tam said, making a quick calculation. "But it would have to be a night ambush, with that few men. A quick, vicious strike. We just might win."

"We jest might get kilt, too," Colly said. But he grinned.

"Colly, I'm not a brave man. But I'm ready to tackle that supply train single-handed if it will defeat Strike."

"Well spoken, Tam," Stephanie Devoe said, stepping out of the shadow. "If Strike would do what he did to a girl, what will he do to our people? He will let them fight until he is through with them, then betray them. When you ride south, I ride with you."

"Shet your mouth, girl," Devoe said. "You better—"

"Papa, be quiet," Stephanie said. "I can ride and shoot as well as any man of the Métis. You taught me. And my heart is as hard. Besides my old debts to pay to Clee Strike, I have new ones. I saw the body of that poor girl. I'll ride with Tam."

"All right, wench, have it your way. How's the gal?"

"Better, I think. She is young and healthy. And I doubt if she was as deeply in love with Clee Strike as she thought. She discovered the animal he was, and her vision of the charming prince was ruined forever. She'll be all right with Sophie. They have become friends, since Sophie cared for her during those first terrible hours."

The thought of Stephanie riding into danger with them was not to Tam's liking. But her mind was made up, and there was no use trying to change it.

"What is our next step?" he asked.

To his surprise, he saw the other three looking to him, as if the mantle of leadership had automatically fallen on his shoulders. It scared him, but in his new determination he did not hesitate.

"All right—Gabriel, tip off your chosen men. We'll rendezvous at the mouth of the coulee, two miles south of here, half an hour after dawn."

# 14

N THE LATE afternoon they were sprawled in the scant shade of some serviceberry bushes on a cutbank high above the Marias—seven of them, the two Laurier boys being posted to watch the trail north and south.

Colly Devoe gnawed a fresh cud from a twist of eating tobacco. He masticated it well, and knocked a grasshopper from a weed stem with unerring aim.

"D'jever stop to think, young Tam, that this whole affair is yore fault?" he asked. "These guns we're waitin' fer, they was bought with yellow gold from your bank."

"My bank?" Tam asked. "Colly, when word gets back I won't have any more job than a jackrabbit. The bank will likely write off Strike's loan to profit and loss, and me with it."

"Why not stay in Montana, then?" Stephanie asked. "There are many opportunities for ambitious young men."

"Such as Cleland Strike, who aspires to be an emperor?" Tam asked. "No, Stevie, it takes brassbound nerve to succeed out here. And I haven't got it."

"I'm serious, Tam," the girl said. Her glance met his and slid away. The color came up a little brighter in her cheeks.

Valier, ignoring their byplay, knocked the dottle from his pipe. "My mind is not easy," he said. "If Strike delivers the guns and the cannon to my people as he promised, they will march. I tried one more time last night to warn Pierre. I could not reach him with any words of mine. His thoughts were far away. He said: 'Gabriel, the palace of the premier will have twenty-seven rooms.

The grand ballroom will run the whole length of the building.' 'And the location of this magnificent structure?' I asked. 'Why, at Fort Calgary, the seat of my government.' 'And M'sieu' Strike, where will he be?' Pierre waved his hand. 'Strike, why, I will buy him off when the tribute begins to come in. The man is mad for gold.' 'And the armies of the Queen?' I asked. Pierre looked at me, and through me. 'Gabriel, you must have faith. After our first victory, thousands will rally to our cause. We can turn aside any blow.' It make me sad. I shook my head. 'Pierre,' I said, 'do not trust the man Strike. He is mos' dangerous.' But Pierre laugh. 'Do not fear, Gabriel,' he say, 'after we have the arms, and the little cannon, I will take care of M'sieu' Strike.' "

Colly Devoe shook his head. "LaCroix is as dangerous in some ways as Strike hisself. Tam, you said it last night. We stop this wagon train of arms, or the whole border goes up in flame like a prairie fire." He stood up, staring down at the ford of the Marias below them, the faint ruts of the old wagon tracks, the open space at each bank of the river, partially reclaimed by weed and brush. "I like your plan, Tam. Let's hash it over one more time."

From the brink of the cutbank, using the land below for its own map, Tam once more outlined the desperate strategy he had conceived. The five men and the girl gathered around, not interrupting, intent on understanding. At the end, Gabriel Valier smiled.

"I think a ver' great general was lost when you became banker instead of soldier, Tam," he said. He raised his rifle, squinting over the sights. "One thing. This is war. Tonight we shoot straight; we aim to kill these men of Strike's. We cannot have mercy, for we are too few. This is the chance these men took when they put up their guns for hire."

In the cool of that evening, they mounted and rode down into the valley. The sun was just setting behind the jagged peaks of the Rockies. Tam stationed his men along the trail, well away from it, each man with his role assigned. At the river, north of the ford, he stationed Devoe, Valier, and Pinsonneault. With Ouellette and one of the Laurier boys, Tam and Stephanie rode through the shallow water of the ford. They did not dare deviate from the narrow track, for above and below the ford lay quicksand. As they came up the bank on the south side, Ouellette dismounted and carefully brushed away the hooftracks. Then, with a wave of the hand, he remounted and rode upstream out of sight, Robert Laurier with him.

Tam and Stephanie rode south. A quarter-mile from the ford, they tied their horses in a thicket. They made their way on foot back toward the ford, plunging through cottonwood and willow. They found a secluded place where they could watch the ford but where the brush screened them from observation. Tam checked his rifle, then stretched out in the long soft grass. He yawned, feeling suddenly weary.

"Sleep for a little while, Tam," the girl said. "I'll watch."

Tam was indignant at her aspersion on his alertness as a fighting man. He grunted dissent. He wriggled, trying to find a more comfortable position. He slapped viciously at a late mosquito. In the deepening dusk, he was acutely conscious of the girl sitting so motionless beside him. He propped himself on an elbow, looking at her in the fading light. Her nearness disturbed him. He could smell the faint perfume of her hair. Ah, he thought, she is a lovely thing, this Métisse girl; nor does her Indian heritage detract from her beauty. Too bad, though, that she is of mixed blood ….

With a flash of self-contempt he thrust the thought aside. Her cheeks were a shade more copper, her hair a deeper black, than those of any of the girls he had known. Yet she was a lady, always gracious and helpful. Now she was risking her very life to save her people from inevitable disaster. What more could man ask of woman?

He found himself comparing her with Dove Demarest. In her own way she was as lovely as his cousin. She was poised and self-contained in a way that Dove would never be. But Dove, sick and beaten now, would brighten in beauty again. He would have to get her home, where she could receive the proper care, the love and affection of her own kind of people. He would find passage down the river for the two of them.

His train of thought struck a dead end. Wonderingly, he became aware of two things. The prospect of traveling the breadth of the land with Dove brought no anticipation of pleasure. Once he would have been breathless at the very thought of such intimacy. Now it left him strangely cold. Beyond that, he was troubled at the thought of Philadelphia. He found he had no desire to go back. Why he wanted to stay here he did not know, for this frontier had given him nothing but buffets and blows and the cold touch of death at the nape of his neck. Perhaps it was because, for the first time in his life, he was his own man. But he knew that here he wanted to stay.

Even in this moment, with certain violence coming this way, he had no wish to be anywhere else. The early stars, winking in the velvet backdrop of the night sky, were brighter here, and larger than any he had ever seen. The gentle sighing of the night breeze, the soft plashing of the river below the bank, made a pleasant symphony.

"Tam! Tam! Wake up!" came Stephanie's urgent whisper. "Here comes Strike's wagon train."

Tam jerked awake, reaching for his rifle. How long he had been asleep he did not know, but he was cold and the muscles of his shoulders ached. The world spun and fell into place.

"How far?" he asked.

"Maybe ten minutes," she said. "It's getting along toward midnight."

"Why didn't you wake me?"

"You were tired," she said simply. When he tried to protest further, she touched his lips with strong warm fingers. "No, Tam. I did so because I wished to do so. Listen, the wagons."

Across the quiet night came the clink of trace chains, the creak of leather, the grind and crunch of steel tires on the gravel of the trail. The first wagon came up the little slope and stopped in the clearing by the river's edge. Behind it came a small group of horsemen, then another wagon, and a third. Half a dozen men rode in the rear guard, the star blaze glinting from the steel of rifle barrels.

"By Harry, here's the ford at last," one of them said. He was not speaking loudly, but the night was so still, he sounded so close, that Tam held his breath. "You been talkin' this ford, and braggin' this ford so long, I thought mebbe you made it up."

"Well, I warn't lyin', was I? Here she is, and she's not more'n hub deep. And all around as quiet as the grave."

"Damn it, Phil, if you don't think of the cussedest ways of puttin' things. You make me shiver."

The man Phil laughed. "You oughtta be ready to turn in your checks, Barney. Tonight or some other night, what's the difference?"

"Because, blast you, I still got some hosses to ride and some whisky to drink and some women to kiss afore they pat me in the face with a Long Tom shovel. And I aim to do some."

"Say, what you need..." Phil began. Then his voice dropped. "Take it easy. Here's the boss."

"What's holding you men up?" Strike's voice demanded. His horse came splashing up out of the stream.

"Is everything all right?" Barney asked.

"Of course it's all right, you fool! Get these wagons moving, one at a time. We've marked the safe line of the ford with white rags on stakes. Stay west of 'em. You get these rigs into quicksand and I'll skin every mother's son of you alive. Roll 'em, now!"

His horse went splashing back into the river. From the seat of the lead wagon a whiplash cracked. The hitch moved, the big wagon surged down the bank to the water. Faintly in the star glow, Tam spotted several riders outlined for a moment at the crest of the bank. Now the second wagon lurched down to the river's edge, and stopped.

Tam rose to his knees, looking out over the river. The second wagon began to move. The two wagon tops made faintly lighter blurs against the dim silver sheet of the river. They lurched on, moving with slow care. Tam touched Stephanie on the shoulder. She knelt beside him. He could hear her excited, rapid breathing. He gripped his rifle.

With a jolting shock, the far bank erupted in flame, the slam of rifle fire. In the dark, coming without warning, the guns sounded like those of a small army.

"Ambush!" a man yelled. Answering gunshots winked from the dark water.

One of the riders near Tam yelled, "Get 'em!" and spurred into the water. Others raced after him. A long cry of pain went up from the ford.

"Now!" Tam said, and pressed Stephanie's shoulder. They slid over the bank. Bent low, they raced for the remaining wagon. It's holding back, Tam thought, seeing the gray bulk of it in the starlight. He ran behind it.

He slammed into someone who recoiled in surprise. Tam whipped the barrel of his rifle toward the spot, felt it smash against flesh and bone. With a moan, the man dropped. Tam jumped over him and clambered up a front wheel, onto the wagon box. With frantic haste, he fumbled for the reins. He found them. He felt rather than saw movement beside him.

"Stevie?" he asked softly.

"Yes. Get this rig moving, Tam!"

He threaded the leather ribbons between his fingers. He had done some coaching, a little tandem driving. But no one had ever taught him how to turn a four-horse hitch on an unknown trail in pitch darkness. He had to learn fast.

Reaching for the whip, he made it sing over the flanks of the leaders, then the wheelers. The teams surged forward. His feet braced against the dash, he bore them hard to the left. Brush crackled and the wagon lurched. He was hardly aware of the man clambering up the side of the wagon, until pistol flame lanced the night. The man yelled, and was gone.

"Good work, Stevie," Tam said between set teeth. He eased the hitch around, fighting for the back trail. It came, and he laid the lash hard onto the teams. They took the trail with a rush, the wagon rocking and swaying. Behind them, shots crashed. Tam thought, that will be Ouellette and Laurier. But he had small time to speculate, trying to guide the frightened horses through the scrub and the rocks, his only marker the faintest of notches in the brush.

He tried to pull the horses down, but they had the bits in their teeth. The wheels slammed over rocks, sparks streaming from the steel tires. The horses laid their bellies to the ground and began to run.

From the edge of the trail, three quick shots flared up at them, blindingly orange. Stephanie fired down, once. There was a scream, and they were past, the wagon climbing up on two wheels, to drop back with a crash. The horses raced faster into the blackness.

The brush fell away. The wagon turned, the lurch almost ripping the reins from Tam's hands. By the crunch of stones, they had lost the road.

"Tam cutbank ahead!" Stephanie cried. "Jump!"

He sensed that she was gone from the wagon. He flipped the reins aside and, reckless of neck or limb, unloaded over the side of the wagon. Brush raked his face but broke his fall. He crashed through the bushes, rolling, to bang up against a small tree. Half dazed, dull with fresh pain, he sat up. He heard the wagon receding across the gravel, then suddenly there was silence. Tam held his breath.

The night opened up in a monstrous gout of flame. The earth rocked. Debris thumped and clattered, ticking through the leaves. Something warm and wet struck Tam's face. In horror he clawed it away. He struggled to his feet, swaying, trying to blink away the blinding glare of the afterimage. The monstrous detonation filled him with awe. Strike had something more than gunpowder in that wagon. Dynamite, perhaps, and the blasting caps next to it.

Then the thought hit him—Stephanie! Panic stabbed at him. With a terrible urgency he ran back along the trail, following the deep ruts the loaded wagon had left. "Stevie!" he called. "Stevie!"

He blundered into brush, caromed from a tree. Then his heart leaped. Her voice came from the night. "Here, Tam. Over here."

He stumbled over rocks. As he caught her in his arms, held her close, he could feel the quivering of her body.

"My God, Stevie, I though I'd lost you!" he said. "Are you all right, girl?"

"I'm alive. I'm bruised all over, my ankle is twisted, and my skin is ripped and slashed by catclaws. But I'm alive." She managed a shaky laugh.

"I can't hear any more firing at the ford," he said. "Lean on my shoulder, kid. We'll go back. Watch out—that last man might still be gunning for us."

He helped her along the trail, the girl with the pistol cocked and ready. Tam moved with caution, having lost all sense of distance. Then, over the rim of the valley, sailed the silver arc of a half-moon. Brush and trees sprang into view in its pale light. They could make out the road.

Stephanie literally stumbled over the man who had fired up at the wagon. He lay at the edge of a clump of bushes, his face a white blur in the moonlight. Tam held a pistol on him, while the girl knelt beside him.

She stood up, shaking her head, a tear bright as a diamond on her lashes. "He's dead, Tam. And I killed him."

"He got what he asked for; he tried his best to kill you. All you can do is pray for him, Stevie."

"I will," the girl promised. As they walked down the trail in the moonlight, Tam saw the girl's lips moving silently, the tears glinting unchecked down her face.

# 15

TAM PULLED Stephanie away from the trail into the brush. Toward them came the clatter of a running horse. Perhaps Stephanie recognized the hoofbeats. She sounded the hoot-owl cry that had once startled Tam at the Devoe cabin. The horse slowed abruptly.

"Stevie! Where are you?" came Colly Devoe's voice.

She stepped out into the trail. "Here, Papa. Tam is with me. We're all right."

Colly swung down from his horse. He hugged his daughter. "Whew! Didn't know if I'd ever see you two again, the way the world blew up. Me'n' the country won't never be the same again."

"We jumped just before the wagon went over a cutbank," Tam said. "There must have been dynamite in the load. What of the other wagons? What of Strike and his men?"

"They fought one wagon through the ford, losin' four men doin' it," Colly said. "We downed the horses on the second rig, and it's stalled in midriver. Strike and his men've taken off up the hill. I think they'll be back. That one wagon is mighty precious to him, now that you blew up one of 'em."

"Did we lose anyone?"

"Pinsonneault took a slug in the leg, but he ain't hurt bad. We all had some close ones, but a miss is as good as a mile, they say. Here, Stevie, up back of the saddle. Tam, you take holt of a stirrup leather, we'll go back a-flyin'. We got to do what there is to do, and get out, before Strike gets organized."

Devoe swung into the saddle, and turned the horse uptrail. Tam grabbed a stirrup leather and trotted beside the horse. He had no wind for talk, no energy. He was footsore and leg-weary by the time they reached the Marias again. He felt like dropping into the soft grass, but he did not.

"Girl, you wait here," her father ordered. "Tam, come along. We got to work over that wagon afore Strike comes hellin' back."

Stephanie slid down from the horse. "I'll get our ponies," she said to Tam, and disappeared into the darkness. Colly tied his horse to a tree.

"Come on, Tam," he said, plunging down the bank. "You ain't sugar; you won't melt."

With some reluctance Tam waded into the current, finding the water cool, almost pleasant. He followed Colly toward the gray blob of the wagon sheet in the moonlight. The water came to his thighs. They reached the end of the wagon.

The dead horses had been cut free. It was a matter of bull work to move the bogged wagon. The men were struggling with poles to turn the wagon downstream. Tam and Colly threw their weight into the effort. Gradually the wagon moved, sucking at the mud under its wheels.

"Here she goes," Colly said, jamming harder. "Now turn her, turn her—more to the right. Now heave. *Heave,* damn it!"

The downstream wheels sagged. The wagon began to lean. Hastily the men heaved at their levers, thrust their weight at the upper side. The upstream wheels came sucking out of the bottom. The wagon held for an instant, then went over into the river with a mighty splash.

"That'll wet down the powder," Tam panted.

"Do more than that," Colly said. "Watch this, son."

The wagon seemed to be sinking deep into the water. But Tam, knowing the water could not be that deep, suddenly understood. He shuddered when he realized how little he had understood of the earlier warning about quicksand. The wagon was half under now. The men turned and waded toward the west bank. By the time they got there, Tam could see only the upper curve of the wagon bows.

"She'll be out of sight by mornin'," Colly said with satisfaction. "Here's Stevie with the horses. We better get on our way. You making it all right, Pinsonneault?"

"*Oui*, she's hurt like bugair, but I'm not stay around here," the Métis said, chuckling.

Hope I can laugh if I get a hole shot in me, Tam thought.

Valier and his men mounted. The party sat waiting. Soon young Laurier came storming across the ford, the spray flying in sheets.

"Strike, he comes riding," the young Métis reported. "With maybe ten men, coming this way. They sneak along wit' care, quiet."

"Then let's get out of here," Tam said. He let Valier and Devoe lead the way. He dropped back, then found Stephanie riding beside him.

For several miles the party rode along the riverbank, heading westerly. The country was rough, but in the main they found a trail of sorts. These men knew the terrain like the palms of their hands, having hunted over it many times. Once Valier turned his horse down the bank, leading the way back across the Marias. The narrow channel was deep here, and Tam's horse was soon swimming, snorting at the unfamiliar element. When they came out on the far side, the valley was gentler, the prairie more open. They crossed a ridge, came out on the flat, and found the well-marked track of the Whoop-Up itself.

Tam welcomed it. He was bone-weary and tired of dodging rocks and brush. He reined slightly, letting Stephanie fall in beside him. They rode on together.

After a while, he asked, "Why so silent, Stevie?"

"Tam, I killed a man tonight. I can't pretend it will be easy to forget."

"It's small consolation, but you must tell yourself that your cause was just, and the man was trying to kill you."

"He was young, Tam. When I think of him being cut off from life so quickly, so finally—Tam, I hate my hand that did the thing."

"Your hand, Stevie, was only an instrument. The foot of that man was set on the path of destruction a long time ago. He could have turned aside, but he did not. He knew what he was doing when he took Strike's gold, and now he has reaped his own sowing."

She said doubtfully: "I suppose you're right. Still, he was a human being. He'll haunt me, Tam; he'll live in night dreams."

He reached out and touched her, a quick firm pressure, for he had no other words. No one could help her think this out.

The lead riders turned off the trail. When they paused at the top of a ridge, he was surprised at the height of it above the surrounding prairie.

In the lambent moonlight, the scene was weird. The soft light disguised and distorted the features of the land, making the blacks of the shadows deep pits. The far hills glowed, as if with an inner fire. And over it all the pattern of the blazing stars etched designs with a clear cold beauty. Tam breathed fast with the excitement of it.

"Listen!" Stephanie said softly.

Below them, the sound stretched and distorted by distance, they heard the thunder of racing hoofs. Three horsemen, six, ten—there was no way of knowing for sure in the muffled warp of the night. They passed and were gone, the sound of their going dying out to the north.

The horsemen on the ridge did not stir for a full five minutes. Then Devoe said: "We'll ride northwest, and try to get as close to our own camp as we can by sunup. Strike'll have his hardcases sweeping the prairie for us as soon as it's light. He'll be raving mad."

"Any chance to intercept that other wagon?" Tam asked.

"He left men with it. And they could have gone any route, once across the river. No, not worth the risk, and we've got to get back. Let's ride, men."

They angled east, away from the Whoop-Up, pushing their tired horses hard. They aimed to miss the Hay Lake camp of the mercenaries to the south. As they rode, almost imperceptibly the night fell away. The sky grew gray to the east; the clumps of sage and bunch grass became visible. The Three Buttes heaved up their huge bulks to the north. The eastern sky turned pink and gray with the coming sun, the prairie green and gray under the hoofs of their horses. From a rolling ridge they looked out over the terrain ahead.

It stretched away, limitless in the pearly light, only the low places patches of blackness still. The sun tipped the range with fingers of fire, and light began to move down the steep slopes of the Three Buttes. The men and the lone woman looked about at one another, seeing with new eyes. They drew apart a little, the camaraderie of the blind darkness no longer needed. Each was his own man again.

Tam followed Stephanie's gaze, pleased to see her smile again. He smiled himself, for this was a motley and battered little band, the men wrinkled and dirty; Pinsonneault with a stained bandage around his leg, sitting on one ham in the saddle to ease the pain of the wound; Colly Devoe, his whiskers a tangle, standing in his stirrups, scanning the prairie to the northwest.

Then, faint over the hiss of the dawn breeze, came the firecracker rattle of small-arms fire. It went on for some time, slackening, dying, coming again sporadically. At last it came no longer.

"Somebody got 'em a reception, over around Hay Lake," Devoe said grimly. "Wonder if it was our people. You Laurier boys, fan out and scout ahead. Ride back hell-for-leather if you see anything. The rest of us better get moving, too."

As they spurred their horses, Stephanie asked, "What could the firing be, Tam?"

"Better wait and see, Stevie. It's got me beat. I just hope none of the Métis went off half-cocked."

"Tam, I'm afraid it could be that," the girl said. "This is too big a game for simple people like them. They are too impetuous. Strike is cold enough and hard enough to goad them into foolish moves."

"Can he do it if he doesn't provide the arms?"

"Remember, there was a third wagon, and he has it. It won't take many guns to start a frontier war, though it might to win it."

"And that's a fact," Tam said, frowning.

They had been riding for more than an hour when Colly held up his hand for a halt. Robert Laurier came riding back at the best pace his weary mount could muster.

"M'sieu's, far ahead, a wagon," the Métis said. "Moving northeast at a good pace, a dozen or more riders with it. Everyone in great 'aste."

"Think we could catch them?" Colly asked.

Laurier shook his head. "The party move like the horses are fresh. With these tired beasts"—he shrugged fatalistically—"we cannot even narrow the gap. M'sieu's, I think those man, he riding toward our camp of the Métis."

Colly swore, his profanity heartfelt and sincere.

"What mischief are they trying now?" he asked.

"I do not know," Gabriel Valier answered him. "But we must ride hard to the camp. We must cut straight across."

"That will take us right by the Hay Lake camp," Tam warned.

"Tam, we cain't help that. Got to do what we must," Colly said, and touched spurs to his horse.

They rode with rifle and pistol ready. The puzzle deepened, for even as they neared the hostile camp the ridges and the swales were empty. It gave Tam an uneasy feeling, as if the very peace of the land harbored something grim and ugly.

When they crossed the tracks of the wagon and its outriders, Gabriel Valier dismounted. He fingered the marks in the sod. When he was in the saddle again, he said, "It is ver' much like the track of the first of Strike's wagons, the one that escaped us last night."

"Then he still has guns," Tam said.

"And will use them," Valier said.

Tam was surprised to know that he was on familiar ground. He had ridden this way once with Stephanie, and now he recognized features of the terrain, small marks, a wash here, an odd bush there. The Métis would laugh at such a simple thing, but Tam was secretly pleased with himself. He was not the tenderfoot he had been short weeks ago.

They angled to the east, turned north again. On the east slope of a rolling ridge, Tam reined in.

"I can't help much at the Métis camp," he said. "But we need to know what happened at Hay Lake, if we can learn I'm going to scout it."

Devoe said: "Not a bad idee. But don't get ketched. Git your squint and hotfoot it after us. We'll head straight fer camp. You, Stevie, what you think you're doin'?"

"I'll stay to keep Tam out of trouble," she said.

"No use to argy with ye, I know that. All right, we'll ride."

They rode up the long slope. When they neared the top, they tied their horses and went up on foot, dodging prickly pear, watching for rattlesnakes. With the newly risen sun behind them, they would be skylighted like cardboard silhouettes if they did not take care. They covered the last twenty feet on hands and knees.

Tam used the thin cover of the gnarled clumps of sagebrush. At the very top of the ridge, he found an opening between two large bushes. Wriggling ahead on his stomach, he parted the grass. He heard Stephanie's quick breathing beside him.

They peered down on the Hay Lake camp, seeing it startlingly clear in the crystal air. There was a bustle of activity, a disciplined turmoil of movement. The sun glinted on rifle barrels, twinkled from brass buttons. Where, Tam wondered, had Strike procured the blue uniforms? Earlier, Tam had seen only the most nondescript of military attire. Perhaps he has been saving these for the big day, Tam thought. Still, these men were fully accoutered, even to the odd-shaped cap that was called a shako.

"Could it be that Major Flagg has turned these men into soldiers so quickly?" Stephanie asked.

Shaking his head, puzzled, Tam stared down. Then, from beyond the tents, came the urgent metallic notes of a bugle. The blue-uniformed men moved toward the center of the camp. Enlightenment burst on Tam. He grabbed the girl's arm.

"Stevie—that's it!" he said excitedly. "Not Flagg. Not Cleland Strike's men. We're seeing the real thing—this is the United States Army! I'm going down there."

"Aren't you taking a chance, Tam?" she asked. "They'll be suspicious of strangers."

"These are regulars," he said. "I'll see the officer in command."

"You go, then," she said. "I'll wait here until you signal that it's safe."

He gave her a look of tolerant understanding, and walked down the hill, his rifle slung over his shoulder by its strap. When he was three hundred yards from the perimeter, three uniformed men came up out of the grass. He went on, waving his arm.

He was still moving toward them when their rifles came up. He called out, unslinging his rifle. Smoke jetted from the muzzles of the soldiers' guns, and lead snapped past him, to hit the hillside. He stopped, only then realizing that he was their target.

He went back up the slope like a startled antelope. He heard more shots behind him, heard a bullet *skree-e-ee!* from a boulder. Then he was over the top of the ridge, pounding down the far side toward the horses. He was untying the reins when Stephanie caught up with him. Panting, the sweat dripping from him, he handed her the reins of her pony.

The girl, he saw, was laughing, laughing so hard the tears were standing in her eyes.

"Oh, Tam, If you could have seen yourself!" she cried.

Mortally offended, he sprang into the saddle and spurred his startled horse into a shambling run.

# 16

AM AND Stephanie rode into the Métis camp in midmorning. It had a strange look, the women and children quiet and subdued; the few men about were mostly oldsters, looking morose and touchy. Even the quarrelsome dogs seemed less obtrusive than usual.

A goup of the Métis were gathered at the center of the encampment. Tam and Stephanie dismounted alongside them. Colly Devoe came to greet them, Gabriel Valier waved a hand, his bearded face troubled.

Tam, his fit of pique long passed, took Stephanie's arm.

Gabriel Valier asked, "What did you learn at Hay Lake, m'sieu'?"

"Got shot at, for one," Tam said. "The whole place looks like it's full of regular Army in uniform. Unless it's one of Strike's tricks."

"No trick," Valier said. "My sister, Sophie, she rode to Hay Lake last night to get the clothing of the girl Dove. She find Strike still away; she sleep in her small tent there, waiting for morning. When she woke up she found the camp in the hands of the Army."

"And where is Strike?" Tam asked.

"He came through this camp an hour ago, as if *le Diable* was close upon his heels."

"And heading north?"

"North," Colly said grimly. "With dam' near a hundred of the Bois Brûlés follyin' him. He passed out repeaters as far as they would reach, the grease still on 'em. LaCroix went with him."

"What the devil could have happened?"

"From what Sophie tells us, and by the sign, as near as I can figger it, the Army had moved in at dawn, all of Strike's men asleep. When the real hardcases looked to Major Flagg to lead the fight, turns out Flagg is on the other side! Well, Strike's hired hands might overrun a handful of Mounties, but they wasn't cottonin' to tackle an army. The ones that didn't surrender, they started seepin' away to the west, makin' their own way. Flagg let 'em go, the way Sophie heard it."

"And when Strike returned?" Tam asked.

"Why, he damn' near got hisself shot. He managed to pick up fresh horses in the excitement, but beyond that, he pulled out of Hay Lake and headed fer this camp lickety-cut. Tam, he ain't give up. With his twenty men and the Métis men, he's going to try to storm the border."

"But Colly," Tam protested, "if Flagg is an undercover agent, he has certainly alerted the Mounted Police. They may not be large in numbers, but they are trained fighting men, and well armed. If the Métis rush them—"

Gabriel Valier broke in. "Many of them, too many, will die. M'sieu's, I cannot stand here while my comrades go to their death under the guns of the Police. Perhaps I can talk reason into their hot heads. But if not, when they die, I, Gabriel Valier, can only die with them."

"A noble sentiment," Tam said drily. "But perhaps we can stop them, if they haven't already joined battle."

"Pierre LaCroix is a great man," Valier said. "But he is not a leader of battles. My people are hotheaded, but they are not complete fools. There will be much parley and argument before they set foot across the border, no matter how hard M'sieu' Strike urges them on. Let us ride now, without delay."

"I told the boy Antoine to bring fresh horses," Colly said. "The three of us'll ride north. I ain't got much hopes, but maybe Gabriel is right; maybe they will palaver a while."

"How is the girl Dove?" Stephanie asked.

Devoe and Valier exchanged quick glances. Devoe scuffed the ground with the toe of his boot. Then he looked at Tam and the girl.

"It's bad, Tam," he said. "Strike knew the girl was here. He made fer our tent first thing, shoved Sophie aside, and picked up your cousin Dove. When he rode north, the girl was in the wagon, along with the exter ca'tridges. Tied up, I think."

Tam felt again the hard hot anger build up in him. "Colly, this time he'll kill her. There's one way left—as God is my judge, I'll not rest until I have killed Cleland Strike."

"Remember what I told you onct?" Colly asked.

"I'm not the green hand I was a few weeks ago," Tam said. "And I'm not afraid."

Antoine brought up the horses. They shifted saddles, and in minutes Tam was riding north with Devoe and Valier at a hard gallop. The pounding hoofs jarred a rhythm along Tam's spine. He thought back to the last time he had slept, and wished he were as fresh as his mount. But they did not dare delay.

The trail they followed could not have been missed. A hundred horses and a wagon had marked the prairie, the trail leading northwest, beyond the most western of the Three Buttes, heading toward Fort Macleod. Had the Métis ridden straight on, across the border, headlong into the roadblock the Mounted Police must have waiting? So far, the three had heard no sound of distant gunfire. Tam felt hopeful. By now he was familiar with the mercurial temperament of the Burntwood men. In addition, he had learned what did not appear at first meeting, that these people were endowed with a native shrewdness not to be ignored.

Tam was sure they had stopped short of the border. If they had, Cleland Strike must touch just the right chord, must appeal to just the right nicety of sentiment, and smoldering anger, and hunger for justice. The common sense of the Métis would otherwise make them stop to think twice before they took the irretrievable step of crossing that invisible line. Certainly the Métis rankled at what they thought injustice; surely they had been treated with scant consideration. But many of them must recognize the desperate character of this venture, how it must be completely successful in itself to draw new and powerful forces to the aid of the insurrection. Otherwise there was no hope for the future but the gallows-tree.

Damn Strike and his dreams of empire! Tam thought.

The sun was high and the wide track freshening, when Colly Devoe raised his hand for a halt. He stood in the stirrups, listening intently. Tam quieted his restive horse and tried to separate some alien sound from the hiss of the wind through the sage. Then there came, faint and sweet across the distance, the notes of a bugle.

Without a word the three turned their horses toward the west.

"Never thought I'd be happy at the idear of meetin' a bunch of sojers," Colly said. "Hope it's a calvalry troop. Infantry ain't no more use in this big country than teats on a boar."

"They say there was a cavalry troop at Fort Ellis," Tam said.

"One, exactly one. Fort Assiniboine, Fort Shaw—them's foot sojers. Been wearin' their dam' boots out, tryin' to ketch renegades and hoss thieves who was ridin'. Never heard nothin' so jassack in my life." Colly spat beyond the rump of his running horse. "Even then, they cain't march until the colonel has sent a telegrapht to Snelling, and Snelling has burned the wire to Wash'n'ton. Then Wash'n'ton has a meetin', and telegraphs back fer more information. 'Bout that time some redskin slopes off'n the reservation, an' first thing he needs is some wire fer a rabbit snare, to keep his meat on his skinny bones. So he clips a chunk outen the middle of the telegrapht line, and nobody kin do nothin' for a few days until they get *that* fixed. Do you wonder that a maniac like Clee Strike dang near takes over the whole shootin' match?"

Tam smiled thinly at Colly's grumbling, too preoccupied to pay much attention. Urgency tugged at him, the helplessness of knowing Dove was in danger. He recalled Stephanie's phrase "Death on the wind." It was true, he could feel it. The moment Strike admitted his grandiose scheme was foredoomed to failure, he would be seeking ways to excuse himself from any fault. Dove's betrayal of the arms shipment would be such an excuse. Strike would wreak his terrible vengeance on the girl.

Quartering to the left, they saw the drifting dust cloud that marked the progress of many horsemen. They were riding north in column, the sun glinting from polished brass and blued steel. Tam felt his heart lift at the sight. Not the fault of these men that they were immobilized by conflicting orders, the victims of confused policy and poor Department planning. These were fighting men who knew their business. And they looked it.

An officer, riding near the head of the column, swung out to meet them. Four troopers dropped in behind him. Tam saw then that it was Chance Flagg.

"Who are you, and where are you going?" Flagg demanded, standing clear of the line of fire of his men.

Tam looked at the single bar of a first lieutenant that graced "Major" Flagg's uniform. He looked at the ready carbines of the four troopers. He raised an open palm.

"We are friends, Flagg. I'm Tam Barrie. This is Colly Devoe, and Gabriel Valier, a leader of the Métis."

"How did you know my name?" Flagg asked sharply.

"A few days ago, I was the herb woman's brother. I made the travois to take Dove Demarest away from Hay Lake," Tam said.

"The hell you were! Dove—where is she? Is she all right?"

Tam shook his head. "We ambushed Strike's supply wagons last night. We got two of them, but he took the third one to the Métis camp and passed out the rifles. He and his handful of men, with nearly a hundred Métis fighters, are riding for the border. And with him, from the Métis camp, he took Dove Demarest."

"The devil, the rotten devil!" Flagg said. "And my men can't intercept him short of the border."

"The Mounted Police were told what is going on?" Tam asked.

"Two days ago, when we were massing our troops quietly, ready to gather in Mr. Strike and all his men. But Major Kingston can muster only a handful of men. If Strike has fired up the Métis, Kingston and his troopers will die. They'll die bravely, but they are dead men."

"Well, settin' here palaverin' ain't doin' no good," Colly Devoe said. "Let's get crackin'."

"Right," Flagg said. He gave an arm signal, and the column broke into a trot. With the four troopers riding behind, the three rode with Flagg to the north. The long snake of the column strung out, the dust of its raising drifting down the breeze. Flagg scribbled a note and handed it to a trooper. The man rode off.

"You think the Métis might hold up at the border?" Flagg asked.

"There's a possibility," Tam said. "Pierre LaCroix is an inspired leader, but he has no idea how to handle a mass of men. And I think he knows it. And he does not like Clee Strike."

"And I don't suppose he delivered all the arms he promised," Flagg said. "Not if you men destroyed two of his wagons. Good work, that. Someday I hope to hear the story of that stroke."

"It was touch and go for a while," Tam said. "But I think you're right about the result. Those who stayed in the Métis camp say the young men were not happy about the shortage of rifles and the lack of the two cannon Strike had promised them. They love the little cannon; they think of them as a talisman of sure victory for some reason. But Flagg, how did you change sides so easily—and so quickly?"

The lieutenant laughed. "Always the same side, Barrie," he said. "Civilians seem to think that the Army is sound asleep. Sir, the Army knows there is dynamite in this country, and on a short fuse. My superiors have many sources of information, good ones. They had wind of Strike's mad plan before it was a month old. So orders went to the Southwest for a lieutenant named Chance Flagg. They fitted him with a faked set of credentials as a cashiered hellion, and palmed him off on Cleland Strike. For five months I sat on that powder keg, sweating every time a new contingent of drifters came into the Hay Lake camp. Man! Am I pleased that phase of it's over!"

"Don't blame ye," Colly said. "But ye sure as all hell waited long enough to spring your leetle trap."

Flagg frowned. "Don't think I'm happy about it," he said. "We missed Strike, and there'll be hell to pay if he and the Métis break across the border. We had the infantry from Fort Assiniboine in position, but there was a lash-up in the orders to the cavalry from Fort Ellis. Telegraph wire down, I think."

"What did I tell ye, Tam?" Colly asked triumphantly.

Tam shook his head. "Some good men may die because of this delay," he said. "But at least you immobilized Strike's army. How did they act when you moved into Hay Lake?"

"How do mercenaries ever act?" Flagg asked with the scorn of the professional soldier. "The enthusiasm leaked out of them in a hurry. I doubt if they ever had *much* enthusiasm for Strike's empire building, and I wonder just how many would have crossed the border with him in any case, with the shadow of the noose beckoning to the north."

"What will happen to them?"

"Not much. The quieter this thing is kept, the better, my superiors think. We'll let these men seep through our loose guard if they wish, and make themselves scarce. Which they'll be glad to do."

"The Army brass a bit tetchy about this thing?" Colly asked.

"Plenty. The last thing they want is a national scandal. Our relations with Canada and Britain are already strained by this affair of Sitting Bull. Imagine what an armed insurrection mounted from American soil would do to international friendships. I tell you, if the Métis have crossed the border, one Chance Flagg, late lieutenant U.S.A., will be emigrating to Australia."

From the rear of the column came a rider, galloping hard. Flagg rode back to meet him. They held a short discussion as they rode, Flagg and the hard-faced man with the two bars of a captain on his shoulder tabs. Finally the captain turned off to the head of the column. Flagg returned to the group.

"The captain says we must hold the Métis from crossing the border," Flagg said.

"If they ain't already long gone," Colly said.

"M'sieu' Flagg, these men of yours—if we come upon my people will you order your men to fire upon them?" Valier asked.

"They are American citizens, most of them," Flagg said. "They have the right to ride where they please, and to bear arms. Only if they try to cross the line, to attack Major Kingston's men, will we be forced to fire on them. As for Strike, I'll hale him into custody like the common thief and murderer he is."

"My people, they might get excite', when they see the soliders," Valier said, frowning. "Some hothead might fire the rifle. Many people could get hurt. Let us ride ahead. I still have influence in the council. If I tell them they are alone, that Strike's army is gone, they may heed my words."

The column moved northeast as the lieutenant considered Valier's proposal. Finally Flagg rode off to confer with the captain. He was gone for some time. When he came back he said: "Captain Flores says it's worth trying. He doesn't want anyone killed if it can be helped. I'm to escort you within sight of the Métis, if they are still there. Then it's up to you."

They rode north as the sun swung down the western sky, pushing their horses hard. Sweat trickled down Tam's back. The solid weight of weariness dragged at him. Under a sky of cobalt and brass, the broken peaks of the main range lay far to their left.

The mass of West Butte, part of that strange triple outcrop from the flat prairie, began to loom large ahead.

Ever and ever Tam listened for the sound of gunfire, but it did not come. They stopped for a minute to breathe the horses, to sip warm water from canteens. Still the wide land was silent except for birdsong and the rasp of grasshoppers and the slurring rush of the light breeze.

They came on the Métis beyond a slight rise. A great wave of relief surged over Tam. He looked down on a scene of confusion, of riders and men on foot milling around a wagon like ants in a broken hill. The canvas top of the wagon was silver-gray in the sunlight: Strike's third supply wagon.

"I pray to God that sweet girl is safe," Flagg said.

"She had better be," Tam said harshly. "Wait here, Flagg. We're going in. Don't move unless there's trouble."

# 17

THE THREE rode toward the milling men, Gabriel Valier a little ahead, Devoe and Tam flanking him. As they rode, Tam found himself in close kinship to these men, closer than he had ever been to friends in his life. It must be, he thought, our singleness of purpose, our genuine determination to keep the Métis from this suicidal rebellion. And I'm not afraid, he thought, wondering a little. Maybe when a man runs scared all his life, there comes a day when he has no more capacity to be afraid. There isn't much place for a coward under this immense and unforgiving sky. But there is room for honest anger.

Now the Métis saw Gabriel Valier. A score of them pulled their horses out of the turmoil and came whooping down upon them. There was excitement in their dark handsome faces, and, Tam thought, something of relief at the arrival of this trusted leader. They swung into a compact group around the three, making no effort to relieve them of rifle or pistol.

"Ze rifles, they are few…" "Strike has not the leetle cannon he promise! …" "They say, the Queen she hang ten Bois Brûlé for every Mountie who is kill…." "Gabriel, I theenk we make dam' fool of ourselves. Come and talk truth." In this spate of excited talk, they rode forward, the Métis opening a lane that led to the wagon.

Near the rear of the wagon. Cleland Strike sat a powerful black horse, which curvetted nervously at the noise and excitement. He looked haughtily at the three down his beak of a nose. His mouth was thin and taut with strain. Tam tried to peer past him into the wagon, but Strike's horse blocked the view. Tam could not tell if Dove was in the vehicle.

As Gabriel Valier rode up, the movement of the horsemen stilled. The excited talk died down to a murmur. The Métis drew back, leaving a half-circle around the end of the wagon. At each side of the wagon were ranged half a dozen men, the last of Strike's army from Hay Lake. They sat their horses uneasily, their hands on pistol butts, their eyes searching for possible trouble.

Now Tam could see Pierre LaCroix standing on foot near the tailgate of the wagon. The Métis governor looked confused and distraught, as if he had been caught up in events beyond his comprehension.

Strike, with the nerve and the impudence of a born showman, took advantage of the silence to point his finger dramatically at the three men. "Here are your traitors!" he cried. "Here are the ones who told the Mounted Police that we march today. Fifteen minutes it will take to shoot them. Then, boys, we'll cross the border. We'll sweep the Mounted Police like rabble before us. By sundown we'll be masters of Fort Macleod and Northwest Canada."

At his motion, his handful of men took a stride forward. But rifle hammers clicked behind the three, and the mercenaries moved back, trying to look as if they had not stirred at all.

A young man of the Bois Brûlé said: "These are our own people. We will hear them. Gabriel Valier has always wise counsel."

Tam was inordinately pleased at being included among the Burntwood men, in this sincere speech. He rode a little to the side, to open room for Gabriel Valier.

Valier singled out Pierre LaCroix, motioned him forward. The governor came ahead hesitantly, still looking like a man whose dreams have turned to dust.

"Pierre," Valier said, with a note of sarcasm, "why do our men stand here leaderless, when the border is so close? Why, we should command half of Canada by this hour!"

"Our scouts found the Mounted Police massed to block the main trails to the north. And this man"—he swung a hand toward Strike—"has brought only half the arms he promised, nor has he brought the two cannon he promised. He says they are coming with his men. Our men have refused to cross the border without them."

"In all of the Northwest, there are not more than a hundred men in scarlet tunics," Valier said scornfully.

"That's what I've been telling them, Valier," Strike said. "They can overrun Kingston's men in a few minutes, and open the way to the free land of the Métis."

"Of couse," Valier went on as if Strike had not spoken, "the Mounties are good fighting men. They will take many of you brave lads with them when they die. And the Queen, she does not like it when one of her lads in scarlet dies in her service. The men who do it will be hunted down, if it takes the next twenty years. And they will end on the gallows. But we can forget that."

"Damn you, Valier, which side are you on?" Strike raged. "Ottawa, nor Windsor either, won't be able to touch an independent nation, one with the secret backing of Washington."

"Ah, he is right," LaCroix said eagerly. "This is a wide but empty land. With our Bois Brûlés, and the troops of M'sieu' Strike, we can hold the frontier until we have set up our own government. Then the United States will recognize us, and—"

"Ah, Pierre, Pierre, ever the dreamer," Valier said. "If the might of the United States is ready to bolster your reckless plan, how does it happen that the Army of that same United States moved in the night on the Hay Lake camp—and now of all M'sieu' Strike's vaunted army, there are only these few here free to march?"

"It's a damned he!" Strike cried. "My men—"

"A he?" Valier asked. He pointed toward the rise of the hill. As if on command, half a dozen men rode into view. Even at that distance the blue uniforms and the brass accouterments could be seen plainly. There was a gasp from the Métis.

"That is the Army," Valier said. "A troop of cavalry is just behind them to the south. A fine war you are fighting, Pierre, when such large bodies of troops can move past you in the night without your sentries knowing about it. Nor did you know that Strike's force had ceased to exist. Oh, your rebellion will go far, Pierre."

LaCroix stared at him with agonized eyes, his face more confused than ever. "What can we do now?" he asked dully.

Strike stood up in his stirrups then and spoke, desperation in his voice. "Don't listen to this man! We can still make ourselves master of the Northwest. I will lead you to your heritage. Men, will you be content with injustice, the government taking your lands, turning your wives and children out to starve in the dead of winter? Men, we must ride, we must fight. I will lead you."

Valier said: "Will you be the first to kill one of the Mounted? That is the way of the wilderness, Strike, not the way of honest men. The law is slow, and sometimes it is imperfect. But the way of the law does not leave men lying dead in the long grass, good men whatever side they are on. Strike, do not ask the Bois Brûlés to spend their blood to make you a king."

"LaCroix, order your men to shoot these three," Strike said arrogantly.

LaCroix, Tam thought, has aged ten years overnight. He saw the governor shake his head.

"Strike, I was an ambitious man, for myself, but mostly for my people. As Gabriel says, I dreamed dreams. I saw the goal so plain, so shining, it seemed within my grasp. Though I knew the kind of man you were, I believed your promises because they fitted into my dreams. But Gabriel says no more than truth. To kill, to take our rights by force—we cannot build a nation on that, when the way of the law is still open to us. The whole world would turn its face against us. No, M'sieu' Strike, the Bois Brûlés have no cause with you. Take your men and go." He stood with eyes averted and lips moving, as if he were praying.

Strike, wild with anger, kneed his horse toward LaCroix. Gabriel Valier raised his arm, his fist closed. The arc of Métis started closing in, to the snick of rifle hammers.

"Strike, for God's sake be careful!" Tam said. "Gabriel, hold the men back—let Strike go. Strike, get your men out before one shot starts a battle."

Strike glanced around him. He saw that his men were backing their horses, facing the Métis, but putting space slowly between them. A burly man who seemed to be Strike's second in command held his ground. Strike said something to him in a low voice. The man rode over to the wagon.

Strike faced the crowd, his head high. "We'll go. We have no stomach for cowards and traitors. But there will be an accounting. Remember, Strike and Company expects payment for every last rifle, every cartridge, that I have delivered. Payment in full— in cash."

Tam gaped at the brassbound nerve of the man. With his world tumbling around him, with complete disaster eroding all his reckless gamble, he still could flaunt that monstrous ego of his. And Tam felt the twist of a strange regret, that the drive and the talent of this man had been so wickedly wasted. He could have gone far, Tam thought. For that matter, perhaps he still would.

Then his pity was driven aside. Strike's lieutenant came riding from behind the wagon, leading a pinto pony. Dove sat the pony on a clumsy squaw saddle, her skirts dragged high on ivory thighs. Her face was dark with the old bruises, and the flame of some new ones. Her hair was a silken, tangled mop around her face. She sat with bent head, not looking around, sick, beaten, her gay spirit humbled.

In spite of himself, Tam drove his horse forward. Instantly the guns of Strike's men were raised. Tam reined in his mount. No sense in committing suicide. That wouldn't help Dove.

"Leave her be, Strike," Tam said. "She wants no part of you any longer."

Strike smiled crookedly. "She's my wife, regardless. Where I go, she goes. What I tell her to do, she does. Right, my dear?"

With cruel force he pulled her chin up. Tears were sliding down her swollen cheeks. Tam saw a dark line of dried blood over one cheekbone. But for just an instant Dove caught Tam's eyes. She made the very slightest of negative gestures. Then she dropped her head turning away from the crowd.

Strike backed his horse away from the wagon. "More than that," he said conversationally, "this woman is my insurance policy. We are riding east. Barrie, if you or the others follow too closely, or if anyone fires at us, this girl dies." He leaned forward, his face dark with rage, taking in all the crowd. "Do you understand that, you half-breed bastards? I'll pay you out for a bunch of stinking cowards, as sure as my name is Cleland Strike. I hope I live to see your faces ground into the dust, your lands taken away, your houses, your saddles, your women and children—" His eyes were as wild as his words.

"Shut up, Strike!" Tam said. "The Métis would be worse off than that in your homemade kingdom. You would have made them slaves. Now get out of here, before you say something that blows the lid off the bitter stew you have concocted. And if you harm Dove, I'll find you wherever you are. And I'll kill you."

"You? You hangdog little counterjumper!" Strike swung his horse, his hand going toward his pistol.

"No, Strike," Colly Devoe said. "Unless you want to die sudden. My advice is the almighty same as Tam's—git goin' before my friends have time to savor the rottenness of your crookedness. If'n they do, they'll skin you alive and hang what's left of you up in the sun fer the magpies."

Tam could feel the change in the Métis. Hostility toward Strike and his men was blazing high in these simple people, their betrayal biting at them, their pride trodden into the dust. Strike must have sensed it as well. He rasped out a single epithet. Jerking his horse around, he took the reins of Dove's pony. With supreme contempt, he turned his back on the Métis, ignoring the threat of the ready guns trained upon him. Not a shot was fired. His men closed in around him. They rode east, the soft dust stirred by their passing drifting slowly away in the light breeze.

"That man will kill Dove, Colly," Tam said between clenched teeth.

"He's made a good start of it already, by the look of the poor thing's face," Devoe said. "We'll wait a bit, then we'll folly 'em. Not too close, either, for that devil meant jest what he said. He'll kill her. And he'd like to suck us in an' put a slug in us, too."

They sat their horses by the end of the wagon, watching the Métis gather in small groups, to argue, to mill about, indecisive. Colly said: "I better tip off the lieutenant. He's likely nervous as a cat by this time." He rode off to the south, and Tam saw blueclad horsemen ride down the slope to meet him. There was a lengthy conference, then Colly came riding back. The cavalrymen turned and galloped south.

"He seen most of what went on," Colly reported. "He'll git the captain to keep an eye on our boys, but there ain't nothin' to be afeered of now. Tam, you'n' me and Gabriel, we busted the back of this leetle war, dang near by our lonesome. I'm proud of it."

"We did have a little help," Tam said drily. "Looks like Valier is going to wind it up."

The grizzled Métis leader waved his hat to secure attention. He spoke in Métis, which Tam managed to follow.

"Men of the Bois Brûlés, we were foolish, listening to lies. Because Strike said what we wanted to believe, we listened. But now, my brothers, we have come to our senses, just in time. Let us go home to our families, our friends, our brothers, and with patience and fortitude work for justice, not by the rifle, but by the slow way of the law. Surely the good God will bring men to the light, and the Bois Brûlés will gain their heritage at last. For brothers, the old ways are done. We can never bring them back, try as we will, dream as we will. There will be justice, if not for us, then for our children or our children's children. Go now, and listen no more to false prophets. And light a candle to St. Anne that you are not lying dead on the prairie this night."

Slowly the Métis began to drift away. Some of the shrewder ones rounded up the teams and hitched them again to the wagon, turning it south. A large group trailed after it, toward the camp they had left that morning. A few rode west, a handful turned to the north, knowing a dozen places where they could slip through the thin red line of the Police, and return to their Canadian homes. At the last, only four men remained, Tam, Devoe, Valier, and Pierre LaCroix.

The Métis governor sighed, as if coming out of a nightmare.

"Will you believe me, m'sieu's, that I was trying to do my best for our people? I did not trust that *cochon*, Strike, but I was arrogant enough to think that I was stronger than the strong man. But, like all our people, I am dreamer. I dreamed of glory, but I pushed aside the certainty of blood and suffering and injustice that must go into our rebel state—and the death and the vengeance that would go into the final destruction of it. M'sieu's, I was the foolish one. How can I make it up to the Bois Brûlés?"

"Pierre, you take it hard, and with good reason," Colly said. "But nobody got killed today. The world ain't turned against the Métis, as it would if today you had massacreed the Mounties. You can still do well by your people. Study how to git your story to Sir John Macdonald hisself, and not git put off by any understrappers. I'm like Gabriel here; I think that one day the world'll see justice done for the Métis."

LaCroix smiled faintly. "You too are dreamer, Colly. Your faith is beautiful, though I am not so certain. Justice is a rare and an uncertain thing. But your way is the only way left. I will consult with Louis Riel, who is gifted with the pen. He and I together will plead the cause of justice for the Métis, in Washington as well as Ottawa. The day of the gun, it is past."

He gave them a little salute, then, with head bowed, he rode alone toward the south. They watched him go, in silence.

Finally Valier said: "May I never see death as close again, until my last hour. For there was death all about us today, m'sieu's. I felt the cold breath of it on my cheek."

"Death, and hell to pay after," Colly said. "Strike would have set the border afire from end to end. Thank God it's over!"

"Not quite, Colly," Tam said. "Remember Dove Demarest."

# 18

WHEN TAM rode east, marking the faint dust drift left by Strike's men, Colly Devoe and Gabriel Valier rode with him. Again Tam felt that lift of comradeship, the bond between men that leads them to deeds beyond price. For ambush or trap could lie anywhere along this trail. But the two men did not hesitate.

"Wonder why he is heading fer West Butte," Colly said.

"Strike is, in some ways, wise," Valier said. "I would guess he cached there, perhaps many weeks ago, emergency arms and supplies. Even money."

"That could be," Tam said. "But since Lieutenant Flagg passed the word to the Mounties, Strike will fight shy of the border. He'll have to skirt south of the Three Buttes. Then my guess is that he'll try to reach Benton."

They rode hard. Lucky the horse is fresher than I am, Tam thought, feeling the grinding weariness in his bones. The blazing sun hammered at him; the glare planted a dull ache behind his eyes. But there was no rest, with Dove's plight urgent and dangerous. Tam hadn't the faintest idea how to rescue the girl. Three of them against Strike and a dozen hardcases. All that could be done now was to stay within reasonable distance of them.

Skirting a stretch of rough ground scarified by runoff, they found a faint trail. The grass was sparse, the prickly pear growing thick and venomous in the raw gravel. The great mass of the butte towered to their left. Tam bore to the north, fearful of overreaching Strike's party.

They crossed a deep coulee, the horses grunting as they climbed the far side. On the ridge, Tam stopped to give their mounts a breather.

Colly Devoe took off his battered hat and mopped his streaming brow with his forearm. "She's a hot one," he said. "I know where there's a spring to north'ard. If we want to water, I misdoubt but what Strike will beat us to it. We won't hit no other water—hey, look there!"

Tam stood in his stirrups. He saw racing toward them a lone rider, the dust spilling in a long roll behind him. A group of others rode hard in pursuit. From it bloomed the gray smoke of gunshots, followed long moments later by the faint splat of the explosions. The first rider bent lower over the neck of the horse and came storming on.

Tam spurred his horse to intercept. He waved his hat in the air as a signal. The rider saw it, turned, looking back to gauge the pursuers. Horse and rider dropped from sight behind a slight rise, then came sweeping into full view. With amazement and joy, Tam saw that the rider was Dove Demarest. He sprang down from his horse.

She brought the pony to a sliding stop before him. He reached up his arms and she leaned from the saddle, falling. He caught her. She threw her arms around his neck, hugging him hard, not wanting to let him go. He hardly saw Colly and Valier ride ahead, rifles ready, to block the backtrail.

"Oh, Tammy, Tammy! Always on hand when I need you! Tam, don't let Clee get me into his hands. He'll kill me."

"Now, now," Tam said soothingly, brushing the straggling locks of hair back from her swollen face. "You're safe now, my dear. How on earth did you get away from them?"

Amazingly, she grinned, though she winced at the pain of it.

"I too remember our amateur theatricals, Tam. I played the role of a girl much more ill, much more dazed and fainting, then I actually was. Tam, I played it to the hilt. We came to a spring over there, and stopped to water the horses. Clee's men began arguing about their pay. They wanted to get it and ride out of the country. They claimed their lives weren't worth a plugged nickel if they stayed here. It got hotter and hotter. Finally one of them threatened Clee. Clee drew his pistol and shot the man dead. It looked like a battle was starting. I took advantage of the fight to ease my horse away. When I was clear, I rode south as fast as I could gallop. They took out after me, but I had a good start."

"All of them?" Tam asked, helping her into the saddle and then mounting his own horse.

"Just Clee and two others. I think the rest of them rode off by themselves. I don't blame them. Clee is like a crazy man."

"Only a maniac would beat a woman as he beat you. How do you feel, Dove?"

"I ache all over, my face hurts terribly, and my—my limbs are chafed raw from that rawhide saddle." She looked at him with those great suffering eyes. "But Tam, I'm tougher than I look. I'm not giving up. I'll live to see Clee Strike hanged."

"Good girl," he said, trying with little success to look away from the long beautiful legs her hiked-up skirt revealed. He spurred a little ahead of her, toward Colly Devoe and Valier, who were sitting their horses, watching with ready rifles.

"Why did they stop?" Tam asked.

"Beats me," Colly told him. "Three of 'em, down there on the flat, well out of rifle range. They seem to be havin' palaver over something."

"Two men," Valier said musingly. "Yesterday an army of two hundred men; this morning twenty; now but two. Money does not buy loyalty, it seems."

"And it isn't even his money!" Tam said, with a shock at the memory of things past. He wondered if there were some way he could recover it. Trust Strike to have it well protected.

The three men, small in the distance, broke apart. The two others wheeled away from Strike. With a certain finality in their bearing, they spurred away toward the southwest. Strike raised his rifle, fired once, apparently missing.

"Not two now, Gabriel," Tam said. "How have the mighty fallen! Wonder what his next move will be."

In answer, Strike jerked his horse around with a cruel hand. He rode north into the broken lower slope of the butte, not looking back.

Dove moaned softly. Alarmed, Tam looked at her, seeing her eyes close, her face grow pale. She swayed in the saddle. He held her.

"We've got to get her to some kind of care," he said. "The Métis camp?"

"Better than anything. Sophie and Steve kin care fer her."

With sudden but firm resolution, Tam said: "The two of you take her back. I'm going after Clee Strike."

Colly Devoe gaped at him as if he doubted Tam's sanity. He said: "Don't be a dam' idjut, Tam. That rattlesnake still has his fangs. You go foolin' around with him, he'll kill you."

"There's too much built up between us," Tam said. "His attempts to kill me, the way he treated Stephanie, and now Dove, the money he has filched from the bank—no, Colly, I'll either have a reckoning from that devil or I'll die in one of these deep coulees. I'm afraid of Strike no longer."

"Nobody said you was," Colly said. "But let Gabriel take the girl back. I'll side you against Strike."

"Tam, come with us," Dove Demarest pleaded. "Don't try to take that terrible man. He'll kill you for sure."

Dove's solicitude, her sureness of Strike's invincibility, stirred anger in Tam. He should have been feeling that weakness of the knees, that churning of the stomach, that the thought of Strike had formerly brought him. But now the familiar panic was missing. Instead Tam felt grim resolution. He would not be turned aside.

"You can do as you please," he said curtly. "I'm going to bring in Cleland Strike." He spurred his horse up the trail, not looking back. When no thud of racing hoofs came behind him, he was satisfied. Tam tried to analyze his own motives, but all he was certain of was that he had to best Strike alone and single-handed, or never have any respect for himself again. I've been late in coming into my own, he thought, but today I play a man's part, or die.

He reached down and pulled the carbine from the saddle boot. He jerked a shell into the chamber, expecting Strike to come to meet him, or at least to await his coming. The man would be full of bitterness and a consuming rage, after the desertion of the last of his cohorts. No better target for venting his anger than a hapless Tam Barrie, riding so rashly toward him.

But some of the cumulative events of the past hours must have put a crack in Cleland Strike's façade of arrogance. Had he learned, Tam wondered, that he was only mortal man, like the other fellow, that all his plans and actions were subject to an immutable fate? That there were men in this world who could not be bought or manipulated or blackmailed? It must have been something like that, for now Strike turned the big black horse and went to the quirt, riding north toward the steep slope of the butte.

Somehow Strike's move did not surprise Tam. But Tam was in a state of almost total exhaustion. He lacked the mental energy to seek reasons or to question motives. He merely kept his horse at a steady pace, reining it into the track of Strike's galloping horse. In this heat, on this slope, Strike was taking an unbearable toll out of the big black. Tam could wait.

He kept on the trail, catching occasional glimpses of Strike as he spurred the black northeast, climbing and climbing the scarp of the butte. Tam eased his horse on the flatter stretches, but by the tracks Strike did nothing of the kind for his mount. The terrain grew rougher, the cover more scant as they climbed.

He saw the black horse storm along a narrow ridge, Strike bent low along its back. Then, suddenly, horse and man were gone. Tam turned cautious then, the carbine ready. He eased the horse along the same ridge. From the brush below a shot spanged, and lead snapped above Tam's head. He winced, hunching low on his mount. There was a rattle of brush, and Strike broke out from a thicket above and beyond, on foot, running sideways along the slope. Tam snapped a shot at the man, but he was gone out of sight, still running.

A thrashing in the brush below led Tam to the big black horse; by the tracks it had pitched from the trail, to roll down the steep bank into rocks and brush. The black was struggling, but one leg was twisted beneath it at an impossible angle. Tam tied his own horse, looking down at the black. He could see the smashed stock of a rifle protruding from the saddle holster. Good. Strike had only his pistol left, then. Reluctantly, Tam raised the carbine and shot the injured horse through the head. Only then did he move out on the trail of Cleland Strike.

He moved cautiously. If he played it right, if he did not get careless and fall into an ambush, his rifle could be the margin of victory. He could stand off and cut Strike down, or convince him that he had no course open but surrender. Tam had a feeling that Strike might decide to come in, to take his chance on the court at Benton. After all, he had once had influence.

He caught a glimpse of Strike running across a barren shoulder of the hill. He fired, and Strike dived into the brush beyond. Tam circled, keeping to the rolling slope as the hillside grew steeper. He came to the foot of a belt of sheer rock.

Strike had already scaled it. Pounding down at him came a hurtling boulder, smashing at rock, thundering through the brush. Tam jammed himself against the face of the bluff, spread-eagled, holding his breath. Another rock struck a ledge above him and bounded out into space like a cannon shell. Tam moved fast along the cliff base, gaining each time a boulder had gone past. Now he found a cleft, and swarmed up it with desperate speed.

At the top he threw himself down behind an outcrop, his heart pounding, the breath whistling in his throat. He laid his head on his arms, sobbing the cool clean air into his lungs. I wonder, he thought, if Strike is as desperately weary as I am. But he must be.

Slowly, strength seeped back into his body. In the thin breeze, the sweat grew clammy under his shirt. He came to his knees, the carbine ready. He peered around the outcrop, seeking Strike. Then he saw him, the man's revolver coming up. Tam fired.

The borrowed carbine threw high, chips flicking from the rock face above Strike. Strike did not miss by so much, his pistol bullet caroming off the rock just beyond Tam, to whine off into space like an angry hornet. Tam scuttled back.

He found another way. It circled back, and skirted some bad ground, but at last it led out onto the slope high above. He could see Strike, edging along the steepening face of the mountain, balancing like a tightrope walker. Tam raised the rifle, but Strike was gone again around a shoulder.

Tam climbed higher, teetered over slide rock, came out just above a broken slope. At the bottom it was nearly vertical, and beyond it the butte broke away toward the north. Tam worked on toward the top of the butte, moving with care on the treacherous footing. He came out on a ledge and saw Strike, well below him. He braced himself, tried to quiet the pounding of his heart, and fired. Rock dust sprang from the cliff edge, and Tam swore. The ill-kept rifle fired only approximately where he aimed it. Before he could lever in another shell and fire again, Strike had caught a root of the bushes and pulled himself to safety.

Tam had two advantages, the longer range of the rifle, and the position he had gained overreaching Strike. He moved along the contour of the hillside, hanging to vegetation, hoping to corner Strike where the whole butte fell away in a single cliff. He came around a buttress of rock and stood up for a better look.

Too late he realized that he had indeed cornered Strike. The man must be hugging the rock on the other side of the buttress, safe below the overhang. Time to bluff, Tam thought.

"That's all, Strike," he called out. "Throw away your pistol and come along with hands up. The hangman is waiting for you in Fort Benton."

Strike's comment was blasphemous and unprintable.

"...nor will a dirty little coward like you take me in," he ended. "I've got a bead on you, Barrie. You'll end here on this butte."

"If you had a bead, I'd be dead now," Tam said. "There wouldn't be any mercy for me from a man who'll beat the life out of a defenseless woman, who will lie and steal, and betray his own men, who orders murder done as easily as he orders his dinner. So come out, Strike. I'm different—I'll let the law take care of you."

Strike sneered. "A man has to make his own law, here on the frontier." He must have moved, for Tam heard the rattle of sliding rock.

"Yours wasn't very successful," Tam jeered, hoping to taunt the man into a reckless move.

Strike cursed again, the tone more bitter than the words.

"I would have carved an empire out of the northwest, except for fools like you, Barrie," he said. "How such a sniveling nonentity as you could wreck my plans. I cannot fathom. You brought in the Army, you turned the stinking Métis against me. I suppose, somehow, you destroyed my arms shipment. Barrie, the time has come for me to kill you."

"Once, Strike, you beat me half to death in front of a girl," Tam said. "Whenever our paths crossed, you made trouble for me. This has been building up a long time, Strike.... But I don't know why I waste time arguing with a common thief."

"Say an uncommon one," Strike jeered. "For $150,000 is a nice haul, even when handed to a man on a silver platter. Too bad I didn't get all of it spent. But after I dispose of you, Barrie, it will be plenty to give me a new start in South America."

"Just over $50,000," Tam said, figuring rapidly.

There was surprise in Strike's voice. "Why, mighty close, fellow. And safe in my own bank, from which I can draw it with ease after I've downed you. You're the only man who knows the story, the only one who would object. Why do you think I tolled you to the top of this hill, like a lamb to the slaughter?"

Rock rattled, and suddenly Tam knew Strike had tricked him. Flame lanced at him from the end of the overhang. The pistol bullet smashed into the stock of the carbine, twisting it out of Tam's grasp, spinning it to the scree below. Tam stood there feeling naked and helpless, unable to move as Strike toiled up the slope, the muzzle of his pistol never leaving Tam. He stopped some ten feet below, bracing his feet in the slide rock, grinning, his cruelty deliberate. Tam felt the sweat of fear cold on his skin.

"I told you what a fool you were, Barrie," Strike said conversationally. "But a lucky fool. The men I sent after you failed for one reason or another—Dirty Nose, Lisbon Frank, Con Aleff, Bryce Flinn. Men are always failing me; none of them ever does anything as completely, as superbly well as I demand of myself. So I led you up this mountain, though I had to change my plan a little when that damned dumb brute of a horse failed me. I'll confess, Barrie, that I was at the end of my rope about the time the last of those filthy renegades rode away and left me alone. But since then my mind has been working. A man like me can't be defeated—he'll always find a way to rebuild. And the first step in my new plan is your death."

Tam braced himself, his mind racing, trying to tie in the chord the name of Lisbon Frank had struck in his brain. And he found it. His hand dropped to his vest.

The hammer of Strike's pistol clicked to full cock. There was a wide smile on the man's face when Tam drew Lisbon Frank's derringer and shot Cleland Strike through the head.

THE *Malcolm Marshall* was a typical upriver steamer. She was small and dirty and uncomfortable. But she was shallow of draft, and with her ungainly grasshopper spars she could cross sandbar and swamp, where the big boats could not go. That was why she was loading for St. Louis at the Fort Benton levee this afternoon in early fall.

Tam considered himself lucky to have obtained passage on her for himself and Dove. He supervised the loading of their luggage into the two cubicles the *Marshall* called cabins, and went out on deck. Dove was standing near the bow. He joined her.

She was looking at the sunbaked little city. "How happy I am to leave this hateful place!" she said, her hand going unconsciously to her cheek, the bruises now fading. Her loveliness was not yet intact, but there was the promise of beauty soon to come. She turned to Tam. "Isn't this a disreputable little boat? But just think, Tammy, every mile downstream will be one mile closer to home."

"So your spirit of adventure is satisfied," Tam said.

"Adventure? Rather say nightmare. Tam, what a headstrong little fool I was—and how I paid for it! I think I'll be perfectly happy in old Philadelphia the rest of my life."

"Life does run more smoothly. But the blood pumps slower, too."

"You want that as I do, Tam, I know. For there was never a drop of the blood of the adventurer in you, Tammy. And with the fine position that will reward you at the bank, for the way you salvaged more than a third of their loan to Clee Strike, you can settle down in comfort to enjoy the finer things of life."

"A vice presidency, perhaps?" Tam asked. "Dove, I'm afraid my exploits out here will hardly recommend me to the sober officers of Seaboard & Continental. The few talents I've acquired in the past months are seldom called upon in financial circles."

"Oh, but I'll see to it that Daddy knows how brave you were, riding alone after that devil, Clee. Tam, I'm glad you killed him." She dabbed at her eyes with a tiny handkerchief. "I loved him once. But for what he did to me ..."

"That's over and done, Dove," he said. "The thing that haunts me is the waste of it, the waste of a man. For I've looked into the cattle business that he played up as the excuse for his loan. It's going to be a great thing. If he had followed it, with his great talents he could have built a real empire, a lawful one. But there was something twisted in the man—I never can forgive his willingness to destroy, perhaps enslave the Métis for his own selfish purpose."

"You love those people, don't you, Tam?"

"I love them as a brother," he said soberly. His hand went to his vest pocket, feeling the crackle of paper there. He knew he would not use it now. But he was tempted, thinking back on the men and women whose paths had crossed his this short summer. And touching his heart the most, the Bois Brûlés the Burntwood people, the gay, innocent ones, caught in the surging wave of the advance of civilization across the wild lands. Would they find justice, or would it ever elude them? Would they yet, in their desperation, try to match force with raw force, and come thereby to the disaster that this year had so narrowly missed them?

"You even acquired for the bank the piece of land Clee had bought as a cattle ranch, didn't you, Tam?" Dove asked.

Tam came back into the present, his hand again touching the crispness of the letter. "It was obviously bought with part of the loan," he said. "The court saw that."

"A pleasant surprise, hearing you two were going downriver on this boat," a voice said behind them. They turned. It was Chance Flagg, trim in blue uniform, the metal gleaming. There was a smile on the man's hard-bitten face.

"Where are you heading?" Tam asked, shaking hands.

"Bismarck and Fort Lincoln, for reassignment," Flagg said.

"Shooting trouble somewhere else, I suppose," Tam said. "Or is there a sinecure waiting for you somewhere because you scotched this dangerous affair without gunfire, and with a minimum of publicity?"

"Little enough I did," Flagg said, smiling. "If the Métis had erupted across the border in a blaze of guns, and killed the Mounties as Strike wanted, the fat would still have been in the fire, and it likely would be Private Flagg of the rear rank."

"And the Métis would be keening for their dead," Tam said.

"Yes, those fine simple people," Flagg said. "But you, Mrs. Strike? You return to Philadelphia?"

Dove held up a dainty gloved hand. "Please, Lieutenant.

Dove Demarest. Not—Not that other. That belongs, as you well know, to a little Cree maiden, in Batoche, across the border."

"My apologies, Miss Demarest," Flagg said, flushing. "And at this late date, may I offer my heartfelt excuses for what I did while you were at Hay Lake? There were times when I would gladly have shot Cleland Strike for the way he treated you. But I had my orders, and I did not dare compromise my hard-earned vantage. I was living in deadly danger as it was, with the chance a deserter might expose me at any moment."

"I realize your position, Lieutenant," Dove said, touching his hand. "And at the end, it was the thing that prevented a war. I understand."

"You understand, but do you forgive?" Flagg asked, his voice serious. With some surprise, Tam realized that Flagg was not asking an academic question. He was genuinely concerned about having the girl's forgiveness.

Tam waited for a tingle of jealousy to touch him. But it did not. He stood watching the two, watching them draw away from him, seemingly unaware that he stood beside them. And pleasant relief flooded him. Dove's broken life was fast mending. It lifted away the responsibility he had unconsciously felt for her future, her withdrawal of her own volition. This Chance Flagg was a good man, one of large capabilities, with something of the qualities Clee Strike might have had with the proper balance wheel.

When Tam stepped back and away, they did not even see him go. He walked down the deck and entered Dove's cubbyhole of a cabin. In the center of the bed he laid the envelope from his pocket. It held her ticket to St. Louis, and a letter. He walked out, closing the door firmly behind him, as if by that act he shut away forever a way of life that once had been his.

He knew now that his mind had been made up last night, or he would not have written the letter. He had deceived himself that the letter was a might-have-been thing, a thing he would never use. His farewell to Dove, that letter. An enclosure held Tam's resignation from Seaboard & Continental, a complete account of the Strike affair, and an offer of Tam's small bank account for the Strike ranch land that would be awarded the bank in due course. He did not doubt the bank would accept the offer.

He got his own luggage from the adjoining cabin. Down the deck Dove and Flagg were still engrossed in conversation. Smiling, Tam shouldered his way past the man at the stageplank. He said: "My plans have changed. Tell the captain I won't be going, and to take good care of Miss Demarest."

"Looks like she's under Army protection," the deck hand said with a knowing leer. Tam laughed, and went on down to the levee.

He had seen them standing back from the river's edge. He put down his luggage and walked toward them. As he approached, he started to speak, but the bull roar of the *Marshall's* steam whistle shattered the air, drowning his words.

When silence surged back, Colly Devoe said: "Whistle means they're gettin' ready to cast off, Tam. Better git back."

Tam's eyes were on Stephanie's lovely face. "I'm not going," he said.

"Ain't goin'? What would ye be doin' out here in the Whoop-Up?"

"Anything," Tam said, taking the girl's hand. "Raise cattle, run a bank, peddle whisky—who knows? But I'm staying."

"But what about that pretty little gal?" Colly persisted. "She ain't goin' to like this one bit."

"She'll make out all right," Tam said, inclining his head toward the two still standing at the bow of the steamboat. "I'll wager she has a proposal from the lieutenant before they reach the Musselshell, and that she accepts him. Good man, the lieutenant. Colly, that girl belongs to my past. And when the boat casts off her mooring lines, the lines to my past are cut as well."

"Not many banks around here," Colly said.

"You think all bank clerks are cowards, like I was? Colly, they're not. Nor do they have to stay so. I'm still a long jump from the bravest individual in Montana Territory, but, by God, I'm not scared of the Whoop-Up. And I'll prove it!"

"Is that the only reason you're staying, Tam?" Stephanie asked, with a childish directness that touched him.

"No," he said, capturing her other hand. "Stevie, this is not the time or the place to say it, but say it I must. Stevie, I love you. Will you be my wife?"

"Tam, I am Métisse. Will my Indian blood shame you in the long days to come?"

"So it showed on me? Stevie, I was a stupid snob, but the Whoop-Up knocked that out of me. I can answer your question now. I will not be ashamed of your Indian blood; and further, there will come a day when I will brag of the Cree ancestors of our own sons and daughters, proud of the fact that they will be Bois Brûlé, the Burntwood people."

Her eyes smiled then, and her lips. With grace and giving she came sweetly into his arms, her beautiful face lifting for his kiss.

They did not hear the shattering bellow of the boat whistle. Only when Colly Devoe tapped Tam on the shoulder did he and the girl draw apart. They saw Colly's lips moving, the words drowned in the blast.

"What's that?" Tam cried.

The whistle stopped suddenly. Colly's words came out in a shout: "Boat's pulling out!"

Tam laughed at him. He put an arm around Stephanie's shoulders, the other across Colly Devoe's massive back. He walked between them to the edge of the levee. From the stern now, Dove waved her handkerchief at them, smiling. She must have guessed, he thought. He lifted an arm to her and Chance Flagg as the *Marshall* walked away from the levee, the white water churning from her sternwheel.

They walked toward the street where Brock, the solid man, waited grinning in the buggy. Tam looked at Colly, then at Stephanie. They were both smiling at him. Why, he thought, everyone knew I was staying except me!

But now I know, he thought exultantly. And he turned away from the river, to look out across the wide free land.

# It's Raining Men

A ROMANTIC COMEDY

## DESCRIPTION

*Don't tell Grandma she's dead.*
*She's still matchmaking.*

"Grandma must have been out of her mind." This is the prevailing sentiment among the four cousins in the Lemont family when they hear that their only heirloom is an ancient umbrella—and each of them must carry it around for three months to receive their inheritance. However, they stick to the rules and soon realize the umbrella has magic powers: When two people share it, they fall in love!

Travis in California, Ainsley in Edinburgh, Carlo in Florence, and Josie in Paris go through the most amazing year of their lives and meet up again a year later. Join the cousins during this tender, amusing, touching and romantic year, and you'll finish their story with a happy feeling deep within.

## PRAISE FOR BEATE BOEKER & GWEN ELLERY

"Ms. Boeker writes heart-warming stories with such fidelity to real life that you will think it might even happen to you."—Romancelover

"Need a lighthearted laugh? Gwen Ellery delivers."—*KD Reviews*

Cover design by Chick Lit Book Covers
Edition: May 2014

It's Raining Men / Beate Boeker & Gwen Ellery

1. Romance / Contemporary—Fiction. 2. Romance / Romantic Comedy—Fiction. 3. Romance / New Adult—Fiction. 4. Romance / Fantasy—Fiction. 5. Romance / Paranormal—Fiction.
I. Title 2014
ISBN 978-0-9912405-1-7 (pbk.)